Relentless Fate

JaQueda Jefferson

Relentless Fate© 2020 by JaQueda Jefferson

This is a work of fiction. Names, characters, places and incidents either are the product of the author's imagination or are used fictitiously, and any resemblance to any actual persons, living or dead, events, or locales is entirely coincidental.

ISBN: 978-0-578-74104-8

This book was printed in the United States of America.

Cover Art Designed by: James Scales Jr.
Editor: Carla M. Dean of U Can Mark My Word
Typesetting: U Can Mark My Word Editorial Services

For additional copies or bulk orders of this book, contact:
jjefferson8ga@yahoo.com

Acknowledgements

There's a story inside everyone.
I hope you're inspired to share yours.

To Paris, Autumn, and all the young storytellers
who I have encountered…I'm listening.

Relentless Fate

Preface

This story, which shares the tale of the struggle of unexpected love, was inspired by the many young people I've encountered who deal with everyday issues involving the evolution of themselves. It addresses survival, love, relationships, teen motherhood, identity, trust, self-knowledge, and drama; it's a story of endurance. I, too, have experienced many of these issues during my younger years. This book is a reflection of many young adults who are living in their truth. As a licensed social worker who has worked with many families and has worked in youth detention for years, I have had firsthand experience with the issues discussed in this book and their effects.

Writing this story wasn't just professional; it was personal. It was important for me to share a story that young adults could relate to and that was relatable to the life they live. I needed to show both sides—male and female. Every perspective is different, but it's important for all young people who pick up this book to reflect on Shay and Kareem's experience that may be similar to their own unexpected love story.

1

"Kareem, get up! Come on, Kareem. I know you hear me!" JaiLynn exclaimed as she pushed her brother's shoulder, trying to wake him up for school.

"If you don't get outta here, I'm going to spazz on you!" Kareem threatened, looking at his sister through squinted eyes while trying to avoid the sun rays shining through the slats of the window shades.

"Are you going to school?" JaiLynn asked, brushing her long, thick hair into a ponytail.

Now wide awake, Kareem wore an annoyed look. His alarm clock had already gone off three times. The two times before he hit the snooze button. The second time the alarm sounded, he had decided then he was not going to school. It was the same ritual every morning, and a constant battle he would never win.

"Naw," Kareem said as he tightened the strings on the du-rag that covered his long, thick braids.

Kareem was still trying to process what had happened at Eddie's cousin's house the night before. Even though he had been there, he didn't understand it. The events that took place had him out of sorts, and he didn't know what to do. The last thing he needed was to get caught up in some stuff that had nothing to do with him.

"Well, Momma is sleep. She said that she's sick and not going to work today. I'm sure you don't want to be around when she gets up," JaiLynn stated with a smirk, cutting her eyes at her brother.

Grabbing the pillow to the left of him, Kareem covered his face with it.

"Out of all days when I want to skip school, she's staying home. Dang, man!"

Kareem tightly clenched the pillow that remained over his face. His breaths became short, and it seemed like he was slowly suffocating himself. He lay there for a minute longer, but that minute felt like forever. Then Kareem slowly lifted the pillow off of his face. JaiLynn, who stood with her hands on her hip and leaning against Kareem's bedroom door, stared at him. She was already dressed, wearing a pair of jeans, a blue, red, and white Polo sweater, and some white Air Forces.

"You're so dumb," she said, shaking her head before leaving his room.

Kareem threw the pillow at her, hitting her in the back of her head.

"Dummy!" JaiLynn yelled as she kicked the pillow into the hall.

Ignoring his sister's comment, Kareem slowly rolled out of bed and trudged to the bathroom. After washing his face and brushing his teeth, he stared at himself in the mirror. He knew his mother would bug out if he did not have a valid reason for not going to school. If he was not dead or in the hospital, she expected him to attend school every day. She didn't care if there was a snowstorm. If it was not declared a state emergency and school was open, he and JaiLynn were expected to be at Cranston High.

Kareem knew better than to get on his mother's bad side. Right now, she appeared to be extra stressed from working double shifts at the hospital. He knew she could explode at any point and lash out from being tired and overworked, and he didn't want to be the reason she did.

A senior in high school, Kareem had no solid plans for his future. At seventeen, Kareem was housed inside a man's body but wore his boyhood on his sleeve. He was a typical teenage boy. He hung out with his friends and flirted with girls but had no real interest in any particular girl.

"Another damn day," he mumbled to himself.

Once he was dressed and ready for school, Kareem walked to his mother's room in the front of the house just off from the living room. He approached her door and knocked lightly.

"Ma," he called from outside her door, but there was no answer.

He knocked a few more times before slowly cracking the door and peeking in the room. His mother lay on her queen-size bed, her dark brown hair a mess and covering her face.

"Ma," he said once more.

"Yes, baby," she mumbled while turning over. She moved her hair out of her face to look at Kareem.

"Me and JaiLynn are about to leave for school. Are you okay? Jai said you were sick. Do you need anything before we go?"

Kareem looked at his mother as he awaited her answer. He knew his mother was not feeling well. She never went to bed without wrapping her hair, and her dark-brown skin was pale. Before speaking, she cleared her throat and took a sip from the water bottle that sat on her nightstand.

"No, I'm fine, Reem. I'm just really tired and not feeling well. I think I caught a bug from work. Can you stop and get me some orange juice on your way back from school?" she requested.

"Sure, Ma. Text me if you need anything else."

Kareem and JaiLynn left out and walked three blocks to the bus stop. They didn't live in the projects; they lived in brick brownstones. All of the kids in the "bricks" met up at the same bus stop on Eliggeston and 56th Street. Everyone from the neighborhood who had to be to work or school by 7:30 a.m. squeezed on the #23 metro bus and rode the 20-minute ride uptown. Uptown was where everyone hung out if they were not kicking it on their stoop. All of the schools, banks, and any store worth going to were located there, too.

"What's been going on with you? Seems like you don't care about much these days. You only go to school when you feel like it. You're lucky you haven't got caught by Ma or kicked off the basketball team," JaiLynn said as they boarded the bus.

Annoyed by his sister's comment, Kareem turned up the volume on his headphones while listening to the music track "Change" from J. Cole's *4 Your Eyez Only* album.

"Mind your business," he told her, then walked to the back of the bus where his boys, Eddie and Donté, were standing.

"Mannn, after last night, I thought you wasn't coming to school," Eddie commented.

Turning down the music, Kareem gave his full attention to his friend.

"I wasn't, but Mom Dukes is at home sick. There's no way I was going to get rashed on. If she finds out I've been skipping school, that's my ass."

Eddie looked at Kareem and shook his head. Donté, the clown and troublemaker of the bunch, was in a trance while holding on to the railing.

"Bruh, you good?" Kareem asked, pushing Donté's arm to break his focus.

"What are you looking at, fool?" Eddie asked him.

"Y'all don't see her?" Donté said, looking in the direction of a beautiful young woman.

"See who? What the hell are you talking about, man?" Kareem asked, looking confused.

Kareem then followed Donté's eyes, and when he saw her, he said to himself, *Who the hell is she?*

As if reading Kareem's mind, Donté said, "They say her name is Shay. You see her sitting next to Chris with his dumpy self."

Chris, who stood about 5'10", weighed 250 pounds and had nappy braids. He wore the same red pointy-toe shoes every day regardless of his outfit. He would wear jeans, a sweatsuit, or slacks with those shoes; Chris didn't care. He always looked like he was going to church with them hot shoes on. The three boys looked at Chris and laughed.

Shay sat staring out the window. Everyone from the bricks could look at her and tell she wasn't from around the area. She looked different, dressed different, and unlike a lot of girls that Kareem was used to seeing at Cranston High, she seemed to be more concerned with coming to school to learn and not to look good for her friends.

How did I miss her? Kareem thought to himself.

They arrived at school and slowly exited the bus. JaiLynn and her friends entered on the freshmen side, while Kareem, Eddie, and Donté went to the opposite side of the building where the seniors entered. Kareem watched Shay go in the same door. It was the first time he had ever seen her. She commanded his attention, and once again, Kareem asked himself, *Where did she come from and when?*

2

"Shhh. Mommy got you," Shay whispered as she tried to rock her 9-month-old son, Jaxson, back to sleep.

Jaxson had been the epitome of Shay's world ever since she gave birth to him. Shay often thought of Jaxson as her new beginning—a fresh start at her already dysfunctional life.

Shay had moved to the neighborhood from Maryland two weeks ago. At first, she was staying with her mother, but things were complicated between them. So, she was now living with Ma, her paternal grandmother. Shay didn't stay with her father because they had never had a close father-daughter relationship. It sucked, and she hated it. But, it was what it was, even though she wished things were different. It would've been nice to have a male figure around for Jaxson since his father was incarcerated in Milvern, twenty miles outside of Richmond.

Convenient, Shay thought, but she knew she could not do anything with a man in jail, who continued to make poor decisions and act like he didn't have to live for his son. She didn't make Jaxson alone nor did she anticipate being a single teenage mother. All the usual promises had been made to her, only to be broken. Therefore, Shay was forced to do what she needed to do for her son. She wasn't trying to be another teen mother living off of government assistance, begging people for their help, or even worse, a teen statistic stigmatized by society's social norms. She was determined to make something of herself for her son.

Living in Richmond was different for Shay. She was away from the majority of her friends and family. The only people she had right now were Ma and Jaxson, but she was convinced everything would work out for the best. Shay knew she had this.

"Ma, I just laid Jaxson back down in his crib. He should be fine for a few hours. All of his stuff is in the fridge," Shay said.

"Alright, baby," Shay's grandmother replied as she sipped her coffee while sitting at the kitchen table watching *Good Morning, America.*

Her grandmother, a retired Metro bus driver, helped Shay by keeping Jaxson during the day while she was in school until Shay could secure childcare.

*****

Walking in Cranston High School was like a fresh start for Shay. She didn't have to worry about two-faced girls. You know, the ones who pretend to be your friend, absorb all of your information, flip it, and then start talking trash about you. Yeah, she knew she had a baby at a young age, but truth be told, she was doing a lot better than them. Shay had a lot of motivation. It was just unfortunate that it was not from her mother. Her son was all the motivation she needed, though.

"Good morning, class. Today, we will begin your entry college essays," Mr. Washington said.

Mr. Washington didn't play. He wasn't your average English teacher either. He graduated from Cornell with a Ph.D., and he reminded them all the time. Having studied psychology and African American studies, he was one of those "anything for my people" type of brothers. Mr. Washington went extra hard when he came across struggling black kids in the neighborhood. It was a fact that he made sure you knew you were somebody before you left his class at the end of the school year.

Shay had only been there for a hot minute, but it was obvious to her that Mr. Washington had it out for a few of his students. Of course, it was the brothers. They didn't like to listen and always got offended when a teacher told them what to do, especially if the teacher was a man.

"Donté Johnson, can I speak to you in the hall, sir?" Mr. Washington called out from the front of the class.

Shay watched as Donté, dressed in dark blue True Religion jeans, a red Trendsetter shirt, and a pair of red and black 12's on his feet, closed his notebook and followed Mr. Washington into the hall. Donté appeared to be one of those cocky dudes that every girl was pressed to be with. He was fly, his gear was on point, and his cut was always tight. To Shay, he was just another boy who sat at the back of the class, probably not paying attention to anything the teacher discussed.

Kareem sat at his desk daydreaming about the many things he was dealing with at home. At this point in his life, Kareem was over going to school. He knew he needed the education, but it was hard to focus on writing, work on equations, be around people he didn't care for, and figure out what he wanted to do with his life while being in school for six to seven hours a day. He was more focused on trying to make money. Things were tight at home. His mother was breaking her back trying to provide for him and JaiLynn, and he was tired of seeing her struggle to make ends meet. His father––that coward—had never really been around. He had been in jail for the past eight years, serving out an armed robbery sentence. It's not like he had been worried about Kareem and JaiLynn before then anyway.

"Kareem Cox, can you report to the main office?" Mrs. Clark spoke over the intercom, breaking Kareem's thoughts.

His science book and notebook fell on the floor.

Dang, what is it now? I don't need this, Kareem thought.

While walking to the main office, Kareem saw Donté in the hall talking with Mr. Washington. He knew it was over at that point.

"Come in, Mr. Cox. How are you?"

"Fine, Mrs. Clark. Yourself?" Kareem asked, unenthused about his visit to the office.

"I'm good, but I could be better. Last night, after the boys' basketball practice, there was an incident. A group of students tried to break into the school store. Do you know anything about that?" Mrs. Clark asked as if she already knew the answer. "The reason why I ask...ummm..." She paused to clear her throat. "Your school badge was found on the floor not too far from the store. I wasn't sure if you happened to be in the area and just lost your badge," she said, adjusting her glasses to focus on Kareem.

"No, ma'am. I have my badge right here. See? That one must be the one I lost a few weeks ago. I was at practice yesterday, but I'm not dumb enough to try to break into the school store. Ain't nothing in there for me. They didn't get in the store, so nothing was stolen, right?" Kareem asked, determined they wouldn't make him a statistic.

"You're right. Nothing was stolen, but we need to try and get to the bottom of this," Mrs. Cox replied, choosing her words carefully so as not to turn this into a liability issue. "Okay, Mr. Cox, you can head back to your class. But, if you hear anything, please let me know," Mrs. Clark added, holding the door open for him.

What the heck! I know I've been a little careless, but doing something like that is dumb. Idiots! Like who would try to pull a stunt like that? What they think was going to be in there, money or something? I ain't tryna get kicked out of school. Only thing in that store is cheap school sweat suits and chump change. Besides that, I would have my momma on my back if I did something so stupid, Kareem thought to himself.

Walking back to the class, Kareem didn't see Donté in the hall anymore. He was sure Mr. Washington asked him the same shit. If they had a question for one of them, they would ask all three of them like they were the three amigos. Before he got to class, Kareem saw the girl, Shay, who Donté was talking about. If Donté hadn't pointed her out, she probably would have gone unnoticed with everything Kareem had going on inside his head. She was coming out of the girls' restroom and walking towards Mr. Washington's classroom.

She was pretty, stood about 5'5", had a beautiful caramel brown complexion, and wavy, shoulder-length, jet-black hair. Kareem walked past her with his head down. Their eyes quickly locked, but neither spoke. She smelled nice—a soft, fresh scent.

"This girl is definitely not from Richmond," Kareem murmured to himself.

Shay's school days were okay. But, honestly, spending time away from Jaxson only gave her anxiety. She always worried about what he was doing, hoping he wouldn't give Ma any problems. Typical thoughts for a new mom. Shay knew Jaxson was still getting used to being with Ma all day. When Shay came home, Ma was always excited to tell her about the new things Jaxson was doing. Now crawling, he was curious about all of the things he saw around the house. After Shay's grandfather, Pops, died of cancer a few years back, Ma had been lonely. So, she was happy to have a baby in the house to keep her company and busy.

As for Shay's father, he would come and go when it was convenient for him. He would show up out of nowhere as if no time had passed, working himself into a full head of steam as he lectured Shay about the dos and don'ts of a teenaged girl. When Shay had enough of listening to her father play the daddy role, a few hard questions would ultimately shut him down, and he was out of there until the urge hit him again to play daddy. The last she heard, he was staying with his new girlfriend and her kids. That man was always finding a woman who had herself together and would make her space *his* happy space. Shay was unbothered by her father, though. Ma had always been supportive of Shay, and being her only granddaughter, Ma always spoiled her.

"Hey, honey. How was your day?" Ma asked Shay as she walked into the house.

"It was good. In Mr. Washington's class, we worked on formulating our college essays."

"Sounds exciting, Shay," Ma said as she played with Jaxson on the living room couch.

"It was, but I'm still tryin' to figure it out. I know I want to go to college for sure. However, being new to the area, I have to look into these schools—find something close to here 'cause I can't live on campus with a baby. I will need to find a job, be in class daily, study, and write papers," Shay responded to her grandmother.

Shay always appreciated the support she had with Ma, who never threw shade at her or made her feel less than she was even though she had Jaxson at such a young age. Ma always made sure Shay handled her business. She encouraged her to always think about her future, and she stayed on Shay about finishing school. Shay's grandmother saw the potential in her that her mother didn't see or didn't want to see. Shay always felt the disconnect between her and her mother had more to do with her father than it did with her personally.

Her mother hadn't hidden her bitterness in regards to Shay's father. Like most single mothers, Shay's mother blamed her lack of motivation and determination on her father. According to her mother, Shay's father took her dreams from her—the things she wanted to be and the things she could have done. Shay couldn't understand if there were things her mother wanted to do, why was she blaming Shay's father for not doing them? As far as Shay was concerned, her mother could do anything she wanted to do. It was on her if she didn't do anything to make her life better. Shay also felt her mother was trying to ingrain the bitterness that she had for her father in Shay, but Shay didn't have time to be bitter. She had a son to raise, and nothing or no one was going to get in the way of what she wanted to do for Jaxson.

This was the reason she loved her grandmother so much. She offered more support than Shay felt she ever got from her mother, especially after having Jaxson. They were cool and all, but once she had Jaxson, Shay felt as though her mother looked down on her—always applying unnecessary pressure, stressing her out, and making things more complicated than they needed to be. It's not like her mother could turn back the hands of time, taking them back to before Jaxson was born. Jaxson wasn't going anywhere, and being hard on Shay wasn't going to change that. Back in Maryland, it's what life was like for Shay.

Bump all that. That's why I came to live with Ma, Shay reflected as she sat with Jaxson in the living room.

After school, Kareem met up with Donté and Eddie at the park. Donté confirmed that Mr. Washington asked him about the school store being broken into.

"Bro, Mr. Washington was really on me about that situation. I told him that we didn't have anything to do with it. He was talking about, if he finds out we did, our asses are going to end up like the rest of the idiots kicked out of school because of some dumb stuff," Donté said as he clenched his bookbag close to his chest.

Eddie looked at him and shook his head. "We ain't that dumb," he said with a chuckle.

"So about last night..." Kareem started. "Man, that was messed up. I'm through going around to your cousin's house. There's always some bull popping off over there, and I ain't with all that. We're going to end up getting killed or caught up in some stuff being over there," he said uneasily.

Kareem, Donté, and Eddie were all still pretty shaken up over the events that occurred the night before. They had ended up going to Jamal's house in the valley, thirty minutes outside the bricks. Jamal was Eddie's older cousin, and while the three of them were at his place, something crazy happened. They were chilling and playing video games, when all of a sudden someone knocked on the door. The knocking turned into banging. Then someone tried to kick in the door.

Kareem and Donté were scared; they didn't know who was at the door or how many people were trying to get inside the house. The two boys hid in a closet while Eddie went to see what was going on.

Moments later, they heard someone say, "You thought we wasn't going to find you, nigga?"

Huddled together in the closet, Kareem and Donté tried not to make a sound while breathing hard. Whatever Jamal was involved in, they didn't want any parts of it. They could hear the beating Jamal was being subjected to. Eddie begged whoever it was to stop beating his cousin, begging for his life. But the faceless, nameless person continued his onslaught of savagely beating Jamal. Eddie later told Kareem and Donté how the dude pistol-whipped Jamal, jacking up his face.

Kareem and Donté were out once they heard the dude leave. Kareem was down for the get down, but he was not trying to die or get caught up in Jamal's mess. That whole situation had him shook because things could have gotten even crazier if Jamal's brothers had been there. All he could think of when he got home was how his mother would have reacted if something happened to him. Kareem knew he couldn't live with that. He wasn't trying to put her through more agony and stress. She had already gone through enough throughout the years dealing with his father. All he kept hearing in his head was, *Watch the company you keep because, at any moment, you can end up being an innocent causality.* His mother reminded him of that all the time.

*****

Before Kareem got home, he stopped at the corner market and picked up some orange juice. He kicked it for a few minutes with Abdul, the store clerk. Abdul and his family owned the mini-mart. Kareem had been going to their store for the past ten years. They were a local family and the hub for a good conversation.

When Kareem arrived home later that afternoon, his mother was sitting in the living room watching Tyler Perry's movie, *Good Deeds*. She looked better than she did that morning when he left for school.

"Hey, Ma. How are you feeling?" Kareem asked as he leaned over and kissed her on the forehead.

"I'm better. Thanks for asking. How are you doing? How was school?" she asked, turning her attention from the TV to look at him.

"It was straight. Same stuff, different day. I can't wait for the school year to be over, though. I'm tired of school. I'm tired of the people, seeing the same things, and not seeing much change."

She looked over at him as she grabbed her comb from off the coffee table and started to wrap her hair.

"Boy, you're fine. You don't know what being tired is or what it feels like. You'll be alright. Plus, you're talking about change, but you have to be the change you want to see. You know that," she replied.

She was right, but Kareem thought his mother didn't understand what he was saying to her.

"Ma, you going to work tomorrow?" Kareem yelled from the kitchen as he looked for something to eat.

"Yeah, I am. Why?" she replied sarcastically, knowing her son too well.

"I just wanted to know," he responded right before JaiLynn came in the living room, interrupting their conversation.

"Ma, you got twenty dollars? I need it for tomorrow," JaiLynn said, sitting on the couch.

"For what, Jai? What do you need twenty dollars for now? I just gave you twenty dollars last week. You're going to have to get a job soon. You're asking for money like you paying bills."

JaiLynn was fifteen years old, the only girl, and the baby. She got everything she wanted. Their mother would talk all the crap in the world and still give the girl whatever she desired. JaiLynn wanted all the nice shoes, girly stuff, and smell good perfume to wear for the clowns in school. They knew better, though. They knew she was Kareem's little sister, and he would put hands on anyone when and if necessary. Kareem couldn't stand her most of the time, but he wasn't going for no dudes trying to get close to her, calling the crib, or even coming to the house. For her little friends who had brothers, Kareem made sure JaiLynn didn't spend the night over at their houses.

Shay was up all night with Jaxson, who was coughing, crying, and restless. He didn't usually get sick, but when he did, she felt so helpless. The next morning, Shay checked his temperature, and it was slightly high. There was no way she was going to school and leaving him with Ma feeling that way. School was important, but her baby came first.

"You taking the baby to the hospital this morning?" Ma asked while putting two teaspoons of sugar in her coffee.

"Yes. Do you mind giving us a ride so I don't have to take that packed bus into town?" Shay asked as she placed some baby wipes and a few extra diapers in the diaper bag. She then tried to comfort Jaxson, who was visibly uncomfortable.

"Sure, honey. Let me drink my coffee and get myself together. Give me about ten minutes, and I'll meet you out front," Ma told her.

Shay buckled Jaxson into his car seat. She was growing anxious because no matter what she tried to do, Jaxson continued to cry, which made her worry more. She felt helpless not knowing how to make him feel better.

"He'll be fine, baby," Ma told Shay as she drove her to the hospital.

"I hope so, Ma," Shay mumbled under her breath.

Shay sat in the front of Ma's car, looking out the window and counting the traffic lights they passed en route. She drifted in and out of hearing Jaxson's cries and listening to Lenny Williams' hit, "'Cause I Love You". Ma was infamous for playing old-time classics in her Cadillac.

Ma dropped Shay off at Sturdy Hospital. It was Shay's first time there, so she didn't know where to go. When Ma asked Shay if she wanted her to stay, Shay told her that she could manage on her own. Shay figured Ma could run some errands since she usually had Jaxson at that time.

Shay checked Jaxson in at the front desk. To her surprise, the nurses worked quickly at Sturdy. Shay didn't know if it was because it was early in the day, Jaxson was so little, or what. But, they had them in and out. Jaxson's nurse was pretty cool; she looked like she was around Shay's mother's age. She had long, dark brown hair, hazel eyes, and wore a nice pair of green Polo glasses. She was fly for a nurse. It was the first time Shay saw a nurse wear Prestos with scrubs. The nurse practitioner told Shay that Jaxson had an ear infection and prescribed him amoxicillin. She also told Shay to give him Motrin to reduce his fever. Being new in town, Shay informed the nurse that she didn't know where to pick up his prescription.

"Here you go, baby. This is the address to the closest Walgreens to where you live," the nurse practitioner said, then asked Shay what school she attended.

Shay replied that she went to Cranston High.

"My kids go to school there, too. My daughter is a freshman; you might not know her, though. But, my son is a senior there and pretty well known. His name is Kareem, and he's one of the star players on the basketball team. He has long, thick braids, is kinda slim, and stands 5'10" tall," the nurse practitioner said, describing him.

"I don't know him. I'm not into sports like that. Plus, I have to make it home to my baby straight after school, so I don't have time to go to any games," Shay responded.

"I understand. I know how it is having kids at a young age," said the nurse. "Well, have a nice day. Your baby will be feeling better soon. Just follow the instructions on the medication. If you have any additional questions, my name is Torrie," she concluded.

Once Nurse Torrie left the room to get the discharge papers, Shay called Ma.

"Hey, Ma. We're all set. They said he has an ear infection," Shay informed her grandmother while taking the discharge papers from Nurse Torrie.

"Okay, baby. I'll be there in about ten minutes," Ma told her.

After dressing Jaxson and gathering their stuff, Shay went to wait for Ma in the front lobby. She felt better knowing it wasn't just an ear infection and nothing more serious with Jaxson.

The phone rang. When Torrie answered, Kareem could tell by the tone of his mother's voice that the call was from his incarcerated father. Every time Kareem's father called, it pissed him off because he would only feed him and JaiLynn a bunch of hopeless promises, such as, "When I get out, I'm going to do this…we're going to do that together…and we'll go there." He would get JaiLynn all excited with his false tales, but Kareem knew better than to buy it.

Kareem's father was always caught up in something. The man had been in and out of jail for as long as Kareem could remember. He broke his mother's heart every time he went back to prison. Kareem felt his father had plenty of chances to get it right, and once again, he failed. This time, his father got caught up trying to be the big dawg slinging dope. He tried to pull a fast one and rob a heavy hitter named Mech. Bad idea, very bad idea. He ended up shooting the dude. You can't rob someone who has ties to the street and think you're not going to get caught.

His sentencing messed his mother up. It was the longest sentence Kareem's father had ever been down for in one sitting, and it made his mother go harder for them. Torrie cried countless nights—hopeless and scared for the lives of her children. Then she picked herself up, enrolled in nursing school, and set herself up in a career so that she and her kids would be good no matter what. Most importantly, they wouldn't have to depend on no one ever again.

Torrie had been working as a nurse practitioner for four years at Sturdy Hospital and secured a part-time job for Kareem in the hospital's kitchen on the weekends. Torrie didn't want Kareem to go down the same path as his father—uneducated, selling dope, in and out of jail, unreliable, and not a good role model for his family. Torrie always reminded Kareem that he was going to be a better man than his father. As Kareem got older, he felt more pressured not to fail his mother. It was a lot to live up to, and thinking about it was stressful for Kareem.

What am I going to do? What do I want to do? Those two questions had been playing over in Kareem's head for months, and he was no closer to an answer than he was when he first started asking himself them.

Before he got too deep in his thoughts, his mother passed him the phone.

"Who is it?" he asked, although he already knew.

His mother gave him that look of disappointment.

"Hey, son," Kareem's father said to him after he took the phone.

"What's good?"

"How are things going? I've been writing to you, but you haven't written me back. I've only gotten letters from baby girl."

Kareem listened, feeling frustrated because he felt like he could have been doing something more important than sitting on the line with him.

"Yeah, I'm good. I have just been busy, and to keep it real, I don't have time to write no letters. I'll see you when I see you. You're the one who made the decision to rob and shoot people, wanting to be 'bout that life. You're a clown, man."

Kareem hung up the phone without so much as saying goodbye. He was angry; he knew how hard it was being a young man growing up without a father. Kids were getting killed left and right. Police felt they had the right of passage to do whatever they wanted and not be held accountable. Oppression, gangs, and violence surrounded the youth in their neighborhoods. These streets weren't made for a Black man.

"This dude left me to fend for myself, and he wants to chat like things is smooth," Kareem said to himself.

Torrie, who was putting the sheets she had folded earlier into the closet, had heard the whole conversation. The pain she felt for her son not having his father in his life was one she couldn't describe. Kareem had supportive people around him, but he needed his father. Learning how to be a man should be taught by a boy's father; that shouldn't be substituted.

"Kareem, I need to talk to you," Torrie said from the hallway.

She knew he wouldn't want to hear what she had to say, but there were things Kareem needed to understand.

Kareem slowly pushed out of his seat and made his way to where his mother was waiting for him. He saw it in her eyes that she was mad at him.

"Yes, ma'am?"

"Let me tell you something, Kareem. I don't care what circumstances your father has found himself in or where he is. He is *still* your father, and you will respect him. Do you understand me?" Torrie stated firmly.

Kareem looked at his mother but didn't respond. Torrie stepped right in front of him, reached for his face, and pulled him close enough to her that he felt her breath on his chin.

"I asked you if you understood me, and don't make me ask you again," she said through narrowed eyes and clenched teeth.

"Yes, ma'am, I understand," Kareem replied, looking at his mother.

"I don't expect to have this conversation with you again. You think because you're taller than me, I won't take something and knock your brains out?" Torrie asked him.

She was angry. It hadn't been Kareem's intent to upset his mother, although he was doing everything he could to not laugh in her face. She was the shortest person in the house and always threatening him and JaiLynn with bodily harm when they got out of line.

"No, ma'am. We don't have to talk about it again."

"Alright then," Torrie responded, turning to go to her bedroom. As Kareem watched her walk away, he decided he would apologize to his mother after she had time to calm down.

*****

The next day, Kareem woke up to his uncle Mike sitting at the foot of his bed. *What is he doing here?* Kareem thought. *He sure does have a way of conveniently stopping by the crib.* Kareem knew his mother probably called him after seeing how upset he was once he had talked with his father.

He sat up in bed and looked at his uncle.

Mike was his mother's youngest brother. He knew how inconsistent Kareem's father was, so he always checked in on him. When his mother couldn't figure him out or when he stayed acted out, mostly when he was younger, Uncle Mike would come through, shutting it down. He put hands on Kareem a few times to put him in check. Kareem hated him for it because he always took his mother's side. However, the older he got, Kareem understood it was nothing but love, and he respected his uncle more. His uncle hadn't always been on the straight and narrow himself, but he figured it out along the way. He went and got his associate's degree in business and then his bachelor's in finance. Now he was a big-time businessman.

"Wassup, nephew?" Mike asked as he stood up and fixed his suit in the mirror.

"Nothing much, Unc. What are you doing over here? Ma called you?"

"You know she did, but I was going to stop through anyway because I was in the area. How are you doing? How's school and ball?"

"Things are straight. Could always be better. I'm just tryin' figure things out. Tryin' to help Ma. It's my last year of school, so I'm under pressure to look into schools and stuff. You know, same bull. Pops called, but I'm all set with him. He needs to figure his life out. I can't do that for him. He's grown. I'm tryin' find my own way in these streets," Kareem expressed as he swung his legs around and placed his feet on the floor.

His uncle hadn't lived the same life as Kareem. Kareem's grandparents were married for years. Despite Mike not being in a single-family home, it wasn't hard for him to relate. He was Black, and he was young once. Mike hadn't always been positive and legit; he experienced a few bumps in his road. Sometimes, Kareem forgot how it was talking to his uncle. Mike was very open and down to earth, and after those ass whoopings that he used to get, Kareem knew if his mother didn't have his back, Uncle Mike did.

Before he left for school, Kareem's uncle invited him to stay at his house for the weekend. Mike told him that he would pick him up after school. He knew Kareem needed time to clear his head, and sometimes all it takes is a change of atmosphere. It was Kareem's weekend off at the hospital, so it was perfect timing for him.

*****

When Kareem arrived home from school later that day, his uncle was in the living room talking with his mother. JaiLynn hadn't made it back home yet because she was at the library studying with her friend, Krystal.

"Nephew, go grab you some stuff so we can head out. It's a two-hour drive up to Philly," Mike told him.

Kareem rushed to get his things and loaded them in the truck. His uncle had one of those big-boss Tahoe trucks, all black everything. Every time Kareem rode in the truck, he felt bound for greatness as he reflected on his uncle's life. Before he headed out, he hugged his mother and kissed her on the cheek.

"I'll call you once I get there," Kareem yelled out to his mother as he walked out the door.

A couple of weeks passed, and Jaxson's ear infection cleared up. To Shay's delight, he was back to his usual self. Ma had been so great helping Shay with him. Jaxson's father, Ronnie, tried to reach out to her a few times. Tired of him having his boys calling her phone and random people texting her, Shay told herself that she was going to pick up the next time he called. That day came, and she finally spoke to him. Besides updating him on his son, Shay felt the conversation was pointless. She didn't want to discuss who she was talking to and if she was dealing with someone in Richmond. That was her business, not his. One would think he would've been more concerned with how it was for her being a single mother. To hear him talk about things that had absolutely nothing to do with Jaxson sent Shay over the top.

"When I get out, can I come to see you?" Ronnie asked.

"You don't need to see me. You need to be worried about seeing your son," Shay snapped back.

He told her that he was wrapping up his time soon. Shay wasn't sure what soon meant, but according to Ronnie, it could be at any time. She was done inquiring about his court case and how much time he had left to serve. Her main priority was making sure she and Jaxson were good.

"Ronnie, is there anything else you want to know? 'Cause if you ain't worried about Jaxson, you're wasting my time," she stated firmly.

"Why you gotta be like that, Shay? You know I love you and want my family, man. You talking to me like I'm some bust-down nigga."

Shay could tell by his tone that he was getting upset, but she didn't care. She felt like he didn't appreciate her as his son's mother, especially if he was continuously making poor choices. The cheating, the lies, and lack of respect—she was over it all. Ma always reminded Shay that she couldn't force a man to do right, nevertheless a young-minded one. Ma told Shay that Ronnie's time would come around, and he would realize all the things he could have done better. She said that the time might come when it was not important to Shay, and she would no longer want to deal with him—when a woman's fed up. Ma also said when a girl makes a choice to have a baby, she instantly becomes a woman. However, for a young boy without proper guidance and knowledge, he had to grow to be a man.

Ma was always right. Shay appreciated the advice she received from her grandmother that she couldn't get from her own mother. Shay tried to be as strong as she could be in her situation, but having someone to understand her and listen like Ma made all the difference.

At school, Shay had been doing as much as she wanted to apply to three schools in the area. She also found a part-time job on the weekends. Ma helped her find the job, which consisted of filing paperwork at a local dental office. Whenever Shay got paid, she always made sure to give Ma a few dollars to show her appreciation for Ma watching Jaxson.   The longer Shay was in Richmond, the more she missed everything back home. Honestly, she missed her little sister, Jaylah, who was fourteen and four years younger than Shay. Despite Jaylah being much younger than her, they had always been close. Shay would talk to her like she was her age, negating their age differences and forcing Jaylah to think more maturely. The two would discuss relationships, Shay's problems with Ronnie, and other things that Shay went through.

Being so far away, Shay always thought about her. She hoped her mother wasn't giving Jaylah any bull and that she was doing good in school. Jaylah's father was in her life, so she had him if their mother started acting up. Shay felt messed up being away from her little sister at a time when Jaylah was thinking about boys, in middle school, taking up school sports, etc. Her sister had always been there for her, so it was only right that Shay be there for her. Shay knew Jaylah missed Jaxson and decided she would have to make time when she and Jaxson could go to see her. Having Jaylah come to Richmond was a no; Shay knew her mother would flip and not entertain the idea.

"Hey, Jay!"

"Oh, my God! I feel like I haven't talked to you in forever!" Jaylah yelled with excitement.

"I know, right!"

They both laughed.

"Girl, it hasn't been that long. How are you, though?" Shay asked. "I miss you."

"I'm good. I tried out for the cheerleading team last week. I'm waiting for them to post who made the team," Jaylah replied.

"That's good. I hope you make it," Shay responded, excited to hear that her sister was involved in different school activities.

"How is Jaxson? I miss seeing him every day."

"He's good. I want to come in a few weeks to see you. Make sure you tell Ma so she'll know," Shay told her.

Shay tried her best to avoid direct communication with her mother after the last time they got into it. Her mother was always ready to cuss somebody out, and Shay didn't like that. She loved her mother to death, but her ways didn't mesh with Shay. The last time they got into it, things almost got physical. That's when Shay decided to go and stay with Ma.

Shay and Jaxson ended up going to see her sister a few weeks after that call. Being back home felt so good. Shay missed Jaylah coming in her room and lying across her bed, being nosey. She was forever in Shay's business. Now, Shay was visiting her, lying across her bed, and asking her about everything going on. Shay was her older sister, so it was her job to be nosey. She was curious to know how life was in Richmond. Jaylah told Shay if she didn't come back soon, she was moving down there because she couldn't stand being away from her and Jaxson. Shay and her sister knew their mother wouldn't like that. Jaylah told her sister that their mother hadn't been too hard on her. She was letting her go out with her friends and stuff. She also told Shay that she had been going to her father's house on the weekends more. Shay looked at her sister's report card that she had taped on her bureau and was happy to see that Jaylah was doing good in school. Then, the conversation Shay had been dreading happened—the conversation with her mother.

"How y'all doing at your grandmother's house?" Shay's mother asked her as she took a seat at the kitchen table.

"We're doing okay," Shay replied while standing at the sink washing Jaxson's baby bottles.

"I hope you ain't running your mouth about what's going on in this house," her mother said.

"No, we don't talk about you," Shay answered.

"Make sure you don't."

"I won't," Shay replied angrily.

Who cared anything about what her mother was or wasn't doing? Shay didn't care, so why would her grandmother?

"Don't forget who you're talkin' to. I'm still your mama," her mother said, pointing at her.

Realizing her mother was looking to pick a fight, Shay didn't say another word. She was too tired to entertain her. She just gathered Jaxson's bottles and left the kitchen.

Shay was only in town for two days, but it didn't take long for people around the way to learn that she was back. Ronnie's sister sent her a message on Facebook.

Hey wassup, Shay! Heard you and my nephew are in town. I hope you bring him by so my momma and me can see him. I think it's pretty messed up that you don't keep us updated on what's going on with him. You just up and left the state. My brother isn't feeling it, and neither are we. Can you call me when you get this?

Shay fought the urge to cuss Ronnie's sister out on Facebook, but she decided not to be petty and entertain her. She thought long and hard about if she wanted to take her son to see Ronnie's family. It wasn't that she felt Jaxson shouldn't see his father's side of the family. Shay just didn't get along with Danielle, Ronnie's little sister. She was eighteen, always had something smart to say, and was always in someone else's business when she needed to tend to her own.

When Shay took Jaxson over to Ronnie's mother's house, they were thrilled to see him. When Danielle made a smart comment about Jaxson looking like Ronnie, Shay thought to herself, *This wench.* Instead of saying what she was thinking, she replied, "That's what happens when you have a child with someone. They look just like their other half." She finished her statement with a roll of her eyes and then focused her attention on Jaxson, who was sitting on his grandmother's lap.

"Y'all don't start that mess today, please," Ronnie's mother said while smiling at Jaxson.

Shay respected what Ronnie's mother said. This visit was for Jaxson to see her; Danielle was just lucky she lived there still.

"When's the next time we're gonna see him, Shay?" Ronnie's mother asked.

"I'm not sure when's the next time we will come visit. But, I can let you know, and we can set up a time to come by."

"Please do, Shay. I want to see him next time y'all come," Ronnie's mother expressed, weeping.

Shay felt bad, but moving to live with Ma was a choice she made to better herself so she could do better for Jaxson. No one understood what she was dealing with being in Maryland. Shay was quiet about her business. Well, at least she tried to be, but she always came across meddling people.

Before they left, Danielle made it a point to inform Shay that Jaxson would be a big brother in a few months, running her mouth about business that wasn't hers to tell. It wasn't something Shay needed or wanted to hear. *This fool can't take care of the one he has, and here he is about to have another one.* Her thoughts were interrupted by Ronnie's mother.

"Why the hell would you go and say that, Danielle?" Ronnie's mother shouted, scolding her daughter.

"It was nice seeing you, Mrs. Clark. We're going to take off now," Shay said as she put Jaxson's coat on, cutting their visit short.

Kareem always appreciated going to his uncle's house. It was such a relief because he had the opportunity to talk with him about his true feelings that he hid from everyone else. It was also a break from school and seeing the same things. Philly was so dope. Kareem loved it! He liked the life his uncle lived. Mike was comfortable, had no children, and was doing what he wanted to do with his life. Mike often told his nephew not to let the streets define who he wanted to be in life. Kareem knew his uncle was right. He told Kareem that he needed to take his situation seriously because he only had one life to live, and it could be taken away from him in the blink of an eye.

After that trip, Kareem knew he needed to figure some things out. He couldn't count on basketball to be his meal ticket. He had to think about life goals and his future, especially if he wanted to help his mother out. He heard Mr. Washington's voice telling him, *Young man, you have to think out of the box. You know how many Black boys dream of making it pro? Do you see the reality of that actually happening? Y'all are out for the same dream. Think about it.*

The first thing Kareem did when he got home from his uncle's house was talk to his mother. It was refreshing to be able to talk with his mother about how he was feeling and how he felt lost with not having his father around to give him the support and guidance he needed. He expressed how he felt about needing to see more black men doing positive things other than his uncle Mike. That comment made his mother sad, just knowing how her son truly felt. She reminded Kareem that he had positive role models around him. Mr. Washington and Uncle Mike were available to him at any time. She told him that he couldn't be stuck on the fact that his father was incarcerated, and it shouldn't stop him from being anything he wanted to be. She went on to tell Kareem that the choices his father had made for himself belonged to him, not Kareem. While listening intently to his mother, he understood what she said.

When he went back to school, Kareem started to take things more seriously, taking advantage of his time to ask the teachers questions and get their opinions on certain things. He used his library time to research different careers that interested him and work on his college applications.

One day when Kareem was in the library looking into different schools, the girl who Donté had pointed out came in. Shay caught Kareem staring at her. Looking at him from the study section, she wondered why he wouldn't nod or speak instead of just staring at her. Kareem wasn't sure if he should speak. He smiled a little, and Shay quickly dropped her head and looked away. It was all awkward, but he found himself staring at her anyway. He did this until he checked his watch and saw it was time for his next class. Kareem gathered his things and took the route that would take him past where Shay sat. While passing by, he noticed she had dropped her pen.

"Excuse me, you dropped your pen," Kareem told her, then bent down to pick it up.

As her hazel-colored eyes locked with his, Kareem thought, *She's so dope.*

"Thank you," she said as she took the pen out of his hand.

He left the library and proceeded to go to class.

Back at home, Shay was still pressed by the news of Ronnie having another baby. His son wasn't even a year old, and here he was about to have a whole new baby. That was crazy to her. Honestly, Shay knew she and the other girl were screwed. Ronnie was still in jail, and his future wasn't looking too bright.

Shay tried to make sure that whatever was going on with Ronnie didn't affect her at school. On her lunch break, she stopped in the library to print her revised college essay. When she walked in, she couldn't help but notice a boy who had a strong resemblance to her son's nurse—Nurse Torrie. After staring at the young man for a minute, Shay thought her son looked like a charmer. When he left, Shay went and printed out a copy of her essay. Shay was looking to study psychology and wanted to run a shelter for single mothers or work with youth in the community who struggled with mental health.

Ma was Shay's advocate, staying on her about getting her essays and other business completed. Part of Shay felt like she was doing this for them— herself, Jaxson, and Ma. They were a team.

Kareem knew the more he applied himself, the more productive he would feel while going to school and playing ball. He started having more conversations with teachers about his interests and the things he would like to do with his future. Mr. Washington, his fifth-period teacher, suggested Kareem complete a career assessment with his guidance counselor so he could create a more precise plan of what he wanted to do. Liz, his guidance counselor, wasn't your average high school guidance counselor. She was noisy as hell and always pressing him, trying to get as much information from him as possible. She often said he was too quiet. Every time Kareem met with her, he thought he was meeting with the real-life Ms. Frizzle from The Magic School Bus. Her energy was never-ending, and her mind was limitless. If you gave her an idea, she would give you the career manual. When Kareem met with Liz, he told her about his interest in doing electrical work.

"Ms. Liz, I thought it would be kind of dope to look into electrical work. Start my own company or something," Kareem said as he looked at the stack of college magazines on Liz's desk.

"That isn't such a bad idea, Mr. Cox. Going to a vocational school for a trade—such as electrical, plumbing, or heating—is a great idea, and I think you will be very successful. I like the fact that you are thinking, young man," Liz responded while furiously typing away on her computer's keyboard.

Kareem sat there feeling pretty good about himself.

"Mr. Cox, I printed out a few documents for you to review at home. Grab them from the printer before you leave."

"Yes, Ms. Liz," Kareem said, then grabbed his bookbag that sat on the floor.

"Hey, your options are endless. Never limit yourself. Ask questions, young man, and explore. Let me know if there's anything else I can do to help you," she told him.

"Yes, ma'am," he responded with a smile.

"You have a good day, and please tell your mother I said hi," Ms. Liz concluded.

Kareem left the office with a sense of direction. Before heading to the gym, he grabbed the papers that Ms. Liz had printed out for him. It was a list of vocational schools that taught the electrical trade.

"Ms. Liz is hella weird at times, but she stays looking out," Kareem said to himself.

While walking down the hall, Kareem ran into Chris, wearing an orange velour sweatsuit and those same damn red shoes. Kareem shook his head while trying not to laugh at Chris as he struggled with some papers in his bag.

"Chris, man, what in the hell do you have on?"

"My suit, dawg. You like it? It's tight, right?" Chris replied, grinning.

"Man, you look like a fool with that bright suit on, and why you got them clergy shoes on with it? Where's yo' kicks?" Kareem asked, not believing Chris actually thought he looked good in that outfit.

"You just hatin', Kareem. You ain't right for that," said Chris.

Kareem laughed. He knew there was nothing anyone could say to Chris about the things he wore to school. Chris thought he was the Puff Daddy of Cranston High. No one could tell him nothing!

"Wassup, man?" Eddie said as Kareem walked into the gym, and the two exchanged a one-arm hug. "What's good? Where you been? Me and Donté were trying to get a hold of you for Mya's kickback that she had on Saturday. It was jumping," Eddie told him.

"I kicked it with my uncle for a few days to clear my head. I needed some time away. Just got a lot going on in my head," Kareem said.

"I understand, dawg. Sometimes space is needed," Eddie responded while grabbing the nearest basketball to him and walking with Kareem to the locker room. Once in the locker room, Eddie and Kareem changed into their basketball shorts and then walked back to the court. Coach Ellis asked to speak with Kareem in his office for a minute.

"I'll meet you on the court," Kareem told Eddie.

Kareem walked into Coach Ellis's office that was bright and loaded with all of the team's trophies. They were on a winning streak, and Coach Ellis made sure he had every championship trophy visible.

"Hey, young man, how are things going with you? We missed you at the game on Saturday. You know you're my star player. We needed you, but we made do," Coach Ellis said to Kareem.

"My bad, Coach. I had to clear my head on a few things, but my bad for not giving you a heads-up. It won't happen again," Kareem promised.

Kareem held his head down from the embarrassment he felt for letting his coach down despite the team winning. He respected his coach because Coach Ellis had helped him with bettering his skills, so he felt like crap for not being on the up and up with him.

"I understand, but it's about being a man and meeting your responsibilities. What if you showed up for the game, and I didn't? I can't leave the team hanging like that. That's why they call it a team, Kareem. One can't do anything without the other. Understand me?" Coach Ellis asked, speaking firmly.

"Yes, sir, I understand," Kareem replied.

"Alright, man, I'm done beating up on you. Next time, let me know something," Coach Ellis told him.

"There won't be a next time, Coach," Kareem said, making a promise to himself and his coach.

As he turned to leave the office, Coach Ellis called after him.

"Hey! You need to give me an extra twenty-five laps for your 'failure to appear' act on Saturday."

"I got you," Kareem called back over his shoulder.

Shay sat on the couch with Jaxson and Ma. They were catching up on the new series *Insecure*. Ma wasn't hip, but she was always interested in watching new shows, especially since the season for *Law and Order SVU* had ended.

"Girl, this show is crazy with all this carrying on they doing."

Shay laughed at her grandmother because her grandmother knew of nothing that was going on. Ma called everyone on the show fresh, especially Issa. She couldn't get the concept down.

"Women in my day weren't doing all this nonsense," Ma commented, turning up her nose.

"Ma, this is that new new. I love this show!" Shay replied, laughing at the main character, Issa, running after her ex-boyfriend, Lawrence. "You gotta respect that type of honesty, Ma. She played him and now wants him back, but he doesn't want to deal with her," she explained to her grandmother. "I'm leaving you to it. There's too much going on. I'm going to bed, baby," Ma told Shay as she walked to her bedroom.

With Jaxson asleep at the end of the couch, Shay focused her attention on watching her show and scrolling down the Facebook newsfeed on her cell phone. While scrolling, she saw much hadn't changed with her old friends back in Baltimore. The same bull. Dudes still thinking they could be players, and girls still looking dumb as hell chasing the same dudes who were dogging them out, knowing they were no good.

Dummy, Shay thought to herself after seeing a crazy post some girl made about her daughter's father. *Why is she putting all of her business on here like that?* Before Shay could catch up with what was going on with Facebook, her phone rang. It was Renee Coolie, a girl who she made friends with from school. The girl was cool, and Shay enjoyed her vibe. So, she didn't mind hanging out with her. Besides, Renee wasn't extra crazy.

"Hey, girl, wassup? What are you doing?" she asked Shay.

"Nothing much, girl. Just catching up on *Insecure*. This episode is too crazy," Shay responded as she chuckled.

"Dang, I need to catch up, too. I've been so busy with working and stuff," Renee responded.

Renee went on to tell Shay that she had been talking to some dude named Eddie.

"Who's Eddie?" Shay asked attentively.

"Girl, he's on the basketball team. You'll know him if you see him. He's always with that dude Donté from your third-period class and that dude Kareem, who also plays for the team," Renee informed her.

"Okay, girl! Check you out! Do you like him? How long have y'all been talking? I don't know him, but I see his friend Donté in class, and the dude Kareem, I see him here and there," Shay replied.

"We've been talking low key for a few weeks now. He's cool. I'm interested in getting to know him better. Girl, you're gonna have to get out more so I can introduce you to some people. You've been down here for a bit and still don't know nobody," Renee ranted.

Shay laughed because her friend was right. But, it was hard for Renee to understand her situation because Renee didn't have a kid. So, Shay moved differently.

"I'll think about it, girl," Shay said. She was indeed interested in knowing more about Renee and that dude.

"Girl, I'm for real. Let's do lunch or something so you can get out. Bring the baby."

Shay thought about it and agreed it would be nice to go out and talk. Renee didn't give off crazy vibes; she came off very genuine. Plus, spring just hit, and Shay thought it would be cool for Jaxson to get out, too.

"Fine, fine," Shay finally responded. "Where you trying to go?"

"Well, they just opened this new Mexican spot in the city. I haven't tried it, but I'm trying to see what it's all about. Plus, they have a nice outside eating area where we can chill and catch up," Renee informed her.

"Bet. How about Sunday at two o'clock?" Shay asked. "I work on Saturday."

"Yes, girl! I'm excited. I can't wait!" Renee yelled through the phone.

Shay was happy, too. She hadn't done much other than go to school and work on the weekends. She hadn't even gone on a tour of the city, so it was nice for Renee to ask her to go out.

*****

Sunday came, and it was a beautiful day. The temperature was about seventy-three degrees—a great day to take Jaxson out. Shay made sure she had everything she needed for the outing with Renee and Jaxson. She packed his diaper bag, making sure to put in a light windbreaker in case it got cool and an extra change of clothes because Jaxson could be very messy when eating. Ma gave them a ride to town because she was going for the afternoon Bible study at the church. She told Shay that she would pick them up, too, if they needed a ride later. While getting out of Ma's car, Shay spotted Renee walking around the corner to the restaurant.

"Hey, girl, do you need help with anything?" Renee asked.

"Do you mind grabbing this bag so I can lock Jaxson in his stroller?"

"Sure. Is this Mr. Man? Shay, he is too cute."

"Yeah, girl, and this is my grandmother, Annie."

"Hi, Ms. Annie. It's nice to meet you," Renee said as she helped Shay get Jaxson's stuff out of the car.

"Hey, honey. Y'all have a good afternoon," Ma responded. Before pulling off, she made sure Shay had everything she needed. "Alright, text me if you need anything. My phone will be on silent while I'm in Bible study."

Shay and Renee sat and talked for what seemed like hours. Shay enjoyed that she had someone her age she could talk to; however, she was a bit apprehensive about how much information to share with Renee due to the things she experienced back home. Shay shared enough to create a good conversation, though. They talked about Ronnie, Shay's big move, and Shay being the new girl at school. Renee was pretty open with Shay, too. She told Shay that she was living with her aunt, Mae, on Brookwood. When

Shay asked why she was living with her aunt and not her parents, although apprehensive herself, Renee shared that she hadn't lived with her mother in years. Renee told Shay that she and her little brother, Marcus, lived with their aunt because their mother wasn't mentally stable to care for them. After six months of being in foster care, they moved in with their aunt and her boys.

Shay was at a loss for words and not sure how to respond to Renee's truth. Shay appreciated Renee more for being so personal. Shay was at a loss for words and not sure how to respond to Renee's truth. Shay appreciated Renee more for being so personal. For Renee to be so vulnerable with her, drew Shay closer to her.

"I can't erase my story. I know I'm not the only one dealing with shit, and that gives me my voice of strength. I'm just learning to deal with my situation. Aunt Mae and Uncle Earl take care of my brother and me, and I appreciate it. I would never discredit them. That's why I'm so open, because Lord knows where I'd be if it weren't for them," Renee explained as she dipped her burrito in the special sauce. "Mmm, this is good, girl. You have to try this," she said as she continued eating.

"Ma says you grow through what you go through, and I believe that," Shay said.

It was Shay and Renee's first time trying Mexican food, and they both loved it. Shay even let Jaxson taste some of the food, giving him little bites of rice.

"So, tell me about this dude you were telling me about the other day," Shay probed.

"Eddie?" Renee asked.

"Yes, girl. Who else would I be talking about? It's not like I know anyone else in that school, especially if they aren't in my class. Even then, I barely know them," Shay told her.

"Well, Eddie and I started talking one day after the basketball game. I brought my little brother to the game with me, and we were waiting for my aunt to come pick us up. All of a sudden, we heard someone yelling, 'Hold the bus! Hold the bus!' I turned around, and it was Eddie trying to make the bus. I had Marcus stall the bus driver until Eddie made it. We were right next to the bus stop, so it was easy for Marcus to tell the driver to wait. When

Eddie walked to the bus, he looked my way, and our eyes locked. It was a wrap, girl. The next day at school, I ran into him again, and we exchanged numbers," Renee explained.

Shay and Renee sat and talked until Ma came to pick them up. Shay told Renee that she would have Ma drop her off so she wouldn't have to get on the bus.

Once back at home, Shay prepared Jaxson for a nap. He was worn out and had already been up way past his naptime. Since Shay didn't go out much, Ma was curious to know how Shay's day had gone.

"I had a good time, Ma. The food was so good, and Renee is really cool," Shay told her grandmother.

"I'm glad you had a good time, baby. It's good for you to get out once in a while. You're still young," Ma said to Shay as she loosened her shoulder-length braids.

13

Kareem lay on his bed, his Beats covering his ears. He was scrolling down his music channels on Pandora, trying to find something to vibe to. He often sat in his room listening to music and reminiscing. He enjoyed that old school rap and often listened to new rappers like J. Cole, Kendrick Lamar, and Common. The one who really got him thinking was his favorite rapper, Tupac. It was his writings like "The Rose That Grew from Concrete" that stimulated Kareem's mind.

It was lines like Tupac's that validated Kareem while he was still in his prime of growing. That rose symbolized Kareem. He was trying to find out who he was and get through a tough place in his life. He often felt misunderstood within himself. Each day, Kareem identified himself as the rose that Tupac spoke of. Tupac's rose stood strong at the end, but in reality, Tupac died. That "huh" thought always played in Kareem's head, but then there were his songs like "Dear Mama" that Kareem valued and made him respect his mother even more.

For a woman it ain't easy trying to raise a man.

"Kareem! Kareem!"

Kareem finally heard his mother over the music in his headphones. He was so caught up in the music that he didn't realize she had been calling his name.

"Yeah, Ma!" Kareem yelled as he removed the headphones and slid his feet into a pair of Nike slides. "My bad. I was in the room listening to music," he said, now standing in the kitchen doorway.

"Baby, take out the trash, please. And tell Jai to come inside and help me get this food started. What do you want for a side, corn or string beans?" she asked.

"What are we having, steak or chicken?" Kareem asked.

"Chicken and rice," she replied.

"Cool. Corn is fine," Kareem replied, then went to his room to grab his sweater so he could take out the trash.

Kareem liked when his mother cooked. She always had him and JaiLynn helping her in the kitchen. Kareem usually cleaned and took out the trash; JaiLynn helped with the sides after their mother cooked the meat. His mother had this thing with making sure that Kareem and JaiLynn knew how to do things for themselves so they wouldn't have to depend on other people for their survival. Torrie didn't play. She made sure her kids knew how to cook, clean, and do laundry. When Kareem was younger, he thought his mother was being slick and making them do those things so that she wouldn't have to do them. However, the older he got, he realized her reason and appreciated it.

JaiLynn was behind her brother when he came back inside the house. She tossed her bag on the couch and went straight to the kitchen where Kareem and their mother were talking. "Hey, Ma. What do you need me to do?" JaiLynn asked as she stood washing her hands at the sink.

"Start the rice, then grab the corn on the cob out of the fridge and put it on the stove, please," Torrie instructed while turning down the oven temperature for the baked chicken.

"Ma, I went and talked with Ms. Liz today. She gave me a list of schools to look into for electrical work," Kareem shared.

"Oh yeah? You finally figured it out? Electrical, eh? That's good, baby. What do you plan to do with that trade?" Torrie asked Kareem, attentive to his input.

She was excited that her son sparked a conversation about his post-education. Lately, Kareem had been quiet and caught up in his thoughts, which made it hard for her to communicate with him. She felt left out, but she knew he was going through the coming-of-age transitions and would come around.

"I'm hoping to start my own business. Get a small business truck, some business cards, and go from there. Ma, I can't see myself working for no one else. I want to do more eventually. But, I think by starting with this trade, I can still make money while thinking about what I want to do long term. Plus, I can help you out with no charge," he said, laughing.

"Mama, you know Mr. Daniels is getting old and stuff. He be forgetting what he be doing half of the time. I don't know, Ma. I don't know," JaiLynn said, and they all started laughing.

"She got a point, Ma," Kareem said, shrugging his shoulders.

It was these moments at dinnertime that they appreciated. When dinner was done, the three sat at the table and caught up with each other about their week. It wasn't something they always did, but Torrie made sure she was home for her kids at dinnertime. She changed her schedule from the 3-to-11 shift to working 7 to 3, often picking up shifts on the weekends. She knew time was important for her kids. She knew her presence was needed.

14

"Girl, I don't know about this," Shay said as she nervously clenched the straps of her backpack while entering the library.

"It will be fine. It's just Eddie and his friend," Renee whispered to Shay as they walked past the librarian's desk.

Renee was meeting up with Eddie to study in the library, and she brought Shay along because Eddie told her that his friend was with him. As usual, Shay was apprehensive about meeting some dude who she didn't know. However, wanting to please her friend, she decided to be a team player. As they walked to the library's study block, Shay's nerves began to get the best of her. It was something about meeting new people, especially guys, that caught her off guard.

"Hey, Eddie," Renee said as she reached to hug Eddie.

Eddie smiled from ear to ear.

"Eddie, this is my girl, Shayla, but you can call her Shay."

"Hey, wassup, Shay?" Eddie said, then offered her a hug, as well.

"My boy, Kareem, is here, too. He just went to the bathroom real quick."

Before Eddie could finish his sentence, Kareem walked up to the group, making Shay even more nervous. Unconsciously, she reached to smooth her hair quickly.

"Hey, my name is Kareem, and you are?" he said to Renee and Shay while holding his hand out to shake theirs.

Both girls told Kareem their names and shook his hand.

"Reem, you're gonna link up and study with Shay. Renee and I are going to chop it up and do some work on the other side of the block."

Shay stood there speechless, trying not to look as awkward as she felt.

"Hey, you want to take a seat?" Kareem asked Shay, trying not to stare at her.

"Sure," Shay said.

She removed her bag from her shoulder and took a seat at the table with Kareem. Shay felt him looking at her.

"What class are you studying for?" he asked.

"I just have to review my college essay and study for my science class with Mr. Howard. What class are you studying for?" she asked him.

Shay looked at Kareem like he was looking at her, and she saw him drop his eyes. Shay was doing something to Kareem that had never happened to him before. Girls flocked to him, and he made them nervous, not the other way around. Shay was different, but Kareem couldn't figure out just yet what made her different.

"I have some math stuff I have to review for Mrs. Henderson's test on Thursday," he replied.

They both went silent before Kareem's curiosity got the best of him.

"Can I ask you a question? Where are you from? I didn't start seeing you at this school until recently, and I know everybody," he said with a smile.

"I'm from Baltimore. I've been down here for almost two months now."

"B-More, huh? That's wassup. What made you come to Richmond?" Kareem asked.

"Something new, I guess," Shay responded.

She was careful not to tell Kareem more than she wanted him to know. He seemed nice, but she didn't know him like that.

Shay pulled out her folder. Kareem did the same. They both quietly sat, reviewing their work. Kareem looked at Shay from the corner of his eyes. The truth was, he was distracted by her and couldn't focus on studying for his test.

"What are you trying to study in college?" he asked.

"Psychology," Shay said, pausing from reviewing her paper.

"What do you plan on doing with that?"

As Shay explained what her plan was after she got her degree, Kareem sat there intrigued with her vision. He never came across a girl at Cranston who had their life that far thought out. He was impressed.

"Yeah, I got things to achieve. I got people counting on me, you know? I'm counting on me," Shay said while flipping through the stacks of papers in front of her.

"Yeah, I know. I know the feeling," Kareem responded as he continued to look at Shay, who was now looking at him in his eyes.

"Why are you looking at me like that?" Shay finally asked, smiling.

"Because you lookin' at me," Kareem answered with a chuckle.

He thought this was a good way to let Shay know he was interested. Their connection was broken when Renee and Eddie came around the corner.

"You ready to go, girl?" Renee asked Shay.

"Yeah, girl, I'm ready," Shay replied, then collected her papers and put them in her book bag. "It was nice meeting you, Kareem. You too, Eddie," she said while looking at Kareem.

Shay watched as Renee hugged Eddie goodbye. Then the two girls left the library and headed to their fifth-period class. Both Eddie and Kareem remained behind in the library.

"Girl, I saw how you were looking at that boy," Renee commented, gushing and wanting to know what Shay and Kareem talked about.

Shay smiled. "He's cool," she replied with a shrug.

"Cool? That's it? Don't play with me, Shayla! Y'all both were looking at each other like y'all could eat each other up."

"No, we weren't! Dang, Renee! He's alright," Shay responded, laughing.

"Um-hum. Whatever, Shay. Remember, you're my girl. You need to get over yourself and have some fun. I'll catch you at the end of the day," Renee said as she stopped at her locker. As Shay continued to walk down the hall to her class, she couldn't stop thinking about Kareem. He seemed laid back and all. Very attentive, she thought. She smiled at the thought of knowing in her heart that he was different.

After class, Shay walked to her locker to put away her history books before leaving for the day. When she opened her locker door, a folded piece of paper fell out. It read:

There is something different about you, Shay. I felt so uncomfortable and comfortable at the same time talking to you. Hit me. 804 674 3230. Kareem

Shay looked around to see if anyone was watching her. She smiled at the words on the piece of paper, then folded it and slid it in her back pocket before walking to the rear of the building to catch the bus.

While walking past the gym, she heard a ball bouncing and saw Kareem practicing. He looked up to see her and ran to the hall, still bouncing his ball, but Shay didn't slow her pace toward the exit.

"Yo, Shay, make sure you hit me up!" Kareem yelled down the hall.

Smiling, Shay looked over her shoulder and walked out the door.

15

"Alright, boys, give me twenty," Coach Ellis yelled as the boys ran suicides up and down the court. "Next week, we play Wilson, and I need y'all to be tight!" he shouted over their moans.

Kareem, Donté, and Eddie ran up and down the court. They hated when Coach Ellis pressed them a week before a game. He drilled them hard, but it was always appreciated at the end of a winning game. However, the next day at school, they would all be sore from being pressed so hard.

"Man, what's good with you and ole girl?" Eddie asked, sipping his water during their break.

"What girl?" Donté asked, feeling left out.

"Shay, fool," Eddie answered.

The two looked at Kareem, who stood there with an uneasy face. He was a bit annoyed that Eddie brought it up in front of Donté, knowing Donté liked her first.

"Well, what *is* up since y'all are supposed to be my boys and ain't telling me nothing?" Donté said, somewhat irritated.

"Dude, chill. Reem came with me to meet this shorty who I just started talking to, and she brought her friend. That friend just so happened to be the girl you was jockin' on the bus," Eddie explained.

"Damnnn, dawg," Donté said, waiting to see what Kareem had to say.

"Ain't nothing up. We talked a little, and that was it," Kareem said, dismissing the subject.

He didn't want his nosey friends to know he was feeling Shay until he knew what was up himself.

*****

Later that evening at home, Kareem thought about Shay. He hoped she would hit him up. He didn't want to seem too pressed, but he liked what he saw in her. Usually, he was on the other side––girls pressed to know what was up with him. Yet, here he was worried about someone who he just met. He chuckled at himself.

The house phone rang as he lay on the couch watching the playoffs. It took Kareem a minute to locate the house phone, which no one ever used unless it was during emergencies. After seeing the number, he knew the call wasn't for him.

"Fuck! Jai, the phone!" he yelled.

"Huh? What are you talking about, idiot?" she yelled from her bedroom.

"Come get the phone, man! It's for you!"

"Who is it?" she replied.

"It's your father, yo! You answering it or not? 'Cause I ain't,'" Kareem said as the phone continued to ring in his hand. JaiLynn ran to get the phone before her father hung up.

"You're such a dummy. What, you forget he was your father before he was mine?" she asked, quickly answering the phone. "Hello," JaiLynn said as she walked with the phone to her room.

Kareem continued to lay on the couch unbothered. It was a commercial, so he used that opportunity to flip through the channels. He got through five channels before his cell phone began to vibrate on the coffee table. He picked up his phone and saw a text from an unknown number.

Hey, wassup? It's Shay.

Kareem smiled at his phone. *I knew she was going to hit me up,* he thought to himself while sitting there with the phone in his hand, unsure of how he should respond.

"Fuck it," he mumbled to himself.

Hey, girl. Wassup with you? he texted back.

Nothing much. Just chillin' at the crib. I contemplated on hitting you up. You're so random. LOL, she texted.

But ya did. So, you're just as random as me, shorty, he replied.

She responded, *LOL!*

Kareem and Shay texted all night. They got to know each other, asking the corny questions you ask when you're first getting to know someone. Questions like, what's your favorite color, when your birthday is, and what you like to do for fun. Shay even told Kareem about Jaxson. She was not ashamed of her son and refused to hide the fact that she had a child when Kareem asked her why she hadn't come to any basketball games.

Shay revealing that she had a son to Kareem threw him off. He was surprised because that wasn't something he would have thought. Most girls would have dismissed the fact that they had a child because they were too busy running the street and trying to be in another dude's face. But, he respected her honesty. She was driven, had a plan, and handled her business in school.

*****

The next day, Kareem was up before JaiLynn. He was feeling himself after texting with Shay all night. His mother had already left for her shift, and when JaiLynn finally got up, she was thrown off by seeing Kareem up so early.

"Is everything okay?" JaiLynn asked as she walked passed Kareem sitting at the kitchen table and smiling at his phone.

Distracted, he missed the question. He was reviewing the conversation he and Shay had the night before.

"Dummy, what are you smiling at, and why are you up so damn early?" she asked, trying to see what he was looking at on his phone.

"Mind ya business, you creep, and go brush your teeth," he said, turning his phone so she wouldn't see his messages.

As JaiLynn walked back and forth from her room to the bathroom while brushing her teeth, she watched Kareem fidget with his phone.

"What you got, a new girlfriend now or something?" JaiLynn asked.

Kareem looked at her and cut his eyes. "No. Didn't I tell you to mind ya business?" he responded, then went to grab his bag from his room.

It was 7:15 a.m., and they had to head to the bus stop if they wanted to catch the Metro and make it to school on time. As usual, Kareem met up with Eddie and Donté on the corner. They talked briefly before the bus arrived. They all got on the bus that was packed every morning; they were lucky if they came across any seats. Kareem walked to the back before stopping after spotting Shay standing in the corner. She stood there with one hand holding

54

the railing that kept her standing as the bus periodically stopped and jerked at each stop. The other hand clenched the strap of her backpack that was on her shoulder. As Donté and Eddie continued to the back, Kareem stopped in front of her, grabbing the same railing she was holding. Kareem placed his hand close to hers.

"Good morning," Shay said as she looked at his hand that was touching hers.

She smiled and moved her hand down. Kareem looked at her and smiled.

"Good morning," he replied.

Their ride to school was silent. There were so many people on the bus that trying to have a conversation with Shay was pointless, as everyone would have been in their business. Kareem looked around the bus and saw that Donté and Eddie managed to come across two seats. He looked towards the front of the bus, only to see JaiLynn staring at him with her friends. When she noticed Kareem was looking at her, she rolled her eyes and continued her conversation with her loud friends. Kareem chuckled to himself.

"What's so funny?" Shay asked curiously.

"Nothing, just my annoying little sister being nosey," he replied.

Shay turned her head to look where JaiLynn sat.

"You gotta love little sisters, huh?" she said to him, then redirected her gaze to looked out the window.

Kareem looked down at Shay as she stared out the window. The fresh scent of her perfume and her beauty kept him close. Despite being in front of her, Kareem thought about Shay. Not about her presence but who she was inspiring to be. He was intrigued. He felt defeated and didn't want to come off as some lame dude sweating her. He liked her but didn't want to make it more evident than it was already.

Shay really wasn't interested in talking to any dudes in Richmond. It wasn't her main priority, but she didn't mind entertaining Kareem. He was the first boy at Cranston to address her; everyone else seemed scared. Plus, he was very persistent. Shay liked how Kareem kept her mind off all the negative things in her life, such as raising Jaxson alone and the BS with Ronnie. He was an escape and kept her mind busy from work.

Getting off the bus, Kareem followed Shay.

"Are you going to meet me in the library fourth period?" Kareem asked as they walked to the side of the building.

"Sure, I'll be there. I have some college applications I have to review before sending them out," Shay responded.

"Bet. I'll see you then."

Throughout her first period class, thoughts of Kareem drifted in and out of her mind. She thought about getting to know him more. She also thought about Jaxson. Shay never talked to anyone seriously after Ronnie, and she often wondered what it would be like to be in a relationship with someone after she had a son. After mentioning to Kareem that she had a child, she thought he wouldn't want to talk to her anymore, but that wasn't the case at all. Dismissing her thoughts, Shay wrote down the notes on the board.

"Alright, guys, y'all need to read chapter six and complete the questions at the end of the chapter," Ms. White, the chemistry teacher, announced to the class.

Shay wasn't a fan of science, but it was a required class for her to graduate. She wrote down her homework assignment, then placed her classwork on Ms. White's desk and exited the room. She walked to the bathroom before heading to the library. The students had four minutes between each class to transition to the next one. In the bathroom, she ran into Kareem's sister. Shay didn't say anything because she didn't know her name.

"Hey, you're the girl from the bus. Are you my brother's girlfriend or something?" JaiLynn asked while they were both washing their hands. "Oh, my name is JaiLynn," she continued before Shay got a chance to answer her question.

"Nice to meet you, JaiLynn. And, no, I'm not your brother's girlfriend. He's just my friend," Shay replied. "Have a good day, JaiLynn," she added, tossing her bag over her shoulder before leaving the bathroom.

JaiLynn stood there pondering her interaction with Shay. *Even if she doesn't know she is, she's something, especially how my brother acts around the house now.*

As Shay walked in the library, she spotted Kareem, who was looking at books in the vocational trade section. He looked up, and his eyes caught hers. They both smiled and walked over to the table that sat in the middle of the study section.

"Hey, how was class?" Kareem asked her, pushing his book to the side.

"It was straight. I can't wait to be done. I saw your sister in the bathroom. She's cute. She asked if I was your girlfriend," Shay told him while pulling her binder out of her bookbag and smiling at Kareem.

"Oh God, I'm sorry about that. You know how little sisters are—nosey and hella weird," he said.

"Right, 'cause mine is nosey as hell, too," Shay responded, and they both laughed.

As they sat in the study hall, Shay took the opportunity to be nosey herself, asking Kareem about his plans for after high school. She was pleased that he had goals for himself and wasn't going to sit around the hood and get consumed by negative energy. She valued any person—especially a man— that took pride in their education. It wasn't something she was used to seeing. Her father barely graduated from high school, and besides her distant cousins, she didn't recall many males close to her going to college. As a young black woman, it was important for her to have a good male role model around for her son. Shay sat there intrigued by Kareem's plans with his trade and his future business. He didn't talk as if he had it all figured out, but he spoke with confidence. And that was impressive to her.

17

Kareem enjoyed the time he spent with Shay. They had become a "thing." Because she had a good head on her shoulders, he wasn't bothered by the fact that she had a son. Furthermore, she had good family support. He was a little shy when he met her son, though. It was new to him. He never kicked it with anyone who had a child, and he knew nothing about being a father. He never understood how a man could lay down with a female, create a child, and then not do what they were supposed to do for that child. It was one of the major reasons he despised his father and appreciated his mother for what she did for him and JaiLynn.

Kareem knew it was important for fathers to be in their children's lives—to help them in school, be present in school meetings, and teach them about their history and how to be productive members of society. Most importantly, fathers should teach their sons how to be men because a woman can't do that. Kareem always felt like he lost so much with not having his father around. Sure, his mother was there, and his uncle always came through. But, having a father to teach Kareem everything he needed to know and encourage him was missed in Kareem's life.

Kareem met Jaxson and Ma when he walked Shay to her stoop one day. It was nothing planned. Ma and the baby were sitting on the porch when they walked up. Shay introduced Kareem to her grandmother and her son. Kareem greeted her grandmother warmly and even picked up Jaxson, which surprised Shay. The way her grandmother was smiling told Shay that she liked Kareem, which couldn't have made Shay happier. Kareem stayed for a few before leaving to go home.

Later that day, while Kareem was sitting at the dinner table with his family, his mother asked him, "Reem, when am I going to meet this girl you seem to be all about now?"

Torrie was curious as she passed the Kool-Aid to JaiLynn. Kareem tried to act like he didn't hear his mother as JaiLynn's eyes pierced through his skin.

"Get out my face, Jai. Dang," he said, irritated.

"I was the one who asked the question, so why you mad at her?" Torrie interrupted.

"Ma, I know her nosey self said something. She's always in someone's business," he said, then bit into his chicken.

"What you think, I'm old or something? You think I don't see you walking around with your eyes always glued to your phone? Every time someone texts your phone, you have to step into another room. You walk around this house with your nose wide open, boy. So, like I said, son, when am I going to meet her?" Torrie asked, looking at Kareem.

He was at a loss for words and couldn't respond. JaiLynn continued to stare at him, not wanting to miss a thing. Kareem began to laugh out loud.

"Why y'all so nosey, Ma?"

"It's my job. So, you going to answer me or not?"

"She isn't my girlfriend…yet. She's just a real special friend who y'all will meet soon," he concluded.

"Mmm-hmm. Ma, is there more rice?" JaiLynn asked, not believing a word Kareem said.

*****

Later that night, as he lay in his bed, Kareem texted Shay and told her how his mother and sister were pressing him about meeting her. They never labeled what they were; they just let it all fall into place. Unlike other relationships he'd had before, he was considering bringing Shay to meet his mother. Maybe because he liked her, but this time, he felt like he had found a genuine friendship.

He even realized the more he spoke to her, his focus and insight on certain things changed. He was more focused on his classwork despite him being over school. He knew he had to get through it to move forward with his plans. He admired her focus, drive, and studious personality. He had never seen someone go hard like Shay besides his mother. That's when he felt himself loving her, but that is something he wouldn't share with her until the time was right. Besides, they were just "friends".

*****

The following day, Kareem met up with Eddie and Donté at the basketball court. Donté felt left out because Eddie was spending a lot of time with Renee, and Kareem was spending more time with Shay. He stayed throwing Shay in Kareem's face because he liked her, too, despite not knowing her and her not knowing who he was.

"Y'all in love and shit. Y'all just forgot about me," Donté enviously expressed as he threw the ball to Eddie.

"Dude, what are you talking about?" Eddie asked, frowning.

"Y'all don't hit me up or ask if I want to kick it or anything anymore," Donté explained.

He couldn't help it; he wanted what his friends had.

"Bruh, chill. You sound like a girl right now. Like can we live? You act like we ain't always going to be boys or something," Kareem said.

"Right, bro. Chill. We just tryin' to live," Eddie told Donté.

Kareem knew Donté was upset about him and Eddie hanging with Shay and Renee. Donté was the type to freak out over separation; he didn't do well with change. He and his mother moved so often before coming to Richmond that his head was all screwed up. When he was in grade school, he went to six different schools in two years. Donté had made and lost so many friends that when he felt like there was a separation between the people he formed bonds with, he started acting differently.

The rest of the evening, Donté continued to make Eddie and Kareem feel guilty about spending less time with him. Neither Kareem nor Eddie thought it was a big deal, but Donté stressed the issue.

In the middle of their game, Kareem's phone rang.

"Hey, what are you up to?" Shay asked once he answered.

"Nothing. Just at the park with Eddie and Donté balling up," Kareem replied, grinning.

"My bad. Stop by when you leave so we can hang out," she told him.

Kareem was happy that Shay called him because it gave him the excuse he needed to leave.

"Alright, guys, I gotta be out. I'll catch up with y'all later. I have to take care of some business," Kareem lied.

He honestly just wanted to be away from Donté for the rest of the day. It was aggravating him that Donté wouldn't get off his back about her.

Kareem left the park and headed straight to Shay's. She only lived ten minutes up the street. Along the way, he stopped by the mini-mart to pick up some gum and snacks.

"Hey, it's Mr. Basketball Player!" Abdul yelled from behind the counter.

"Hey, man! Wassup?" Kareem asked as he carried his snacks to the front of the store.

"Nothing, man, besides these little fucks that think they can come in my store and steal when they get out of school. They have another thing coming."

"Man, you're crazy," Kareem said, laughing as he paid for his stuff.

18

Both Ma and Jaxson took a liking to Kareem. The more he came around, the more Shay appreciated his presence. Shay couldn't help but brag to Renee about him.

"Girl, things are really going well. We ain't put no title or anything on it, but his actions are speaking loud," Shay told her as they spoke on the phone.

"That's wassup, girl. "'Bout time you're opening up to someone again," Renee replied.

"It's different, maybe because we are good friends. Everything else just comes naturally. He's supposed to be coming by when he leaves the park with Donté and Eddie. Speaking of, how are you and Eddie doing?" Shay asked.

"Shay, that's my boo. We official and all. He's just how I like 'em. He's smart and down for whatever," Renee replied.

Shay could see the smile on Renee's face through the phone.

"Good for you, girl. If you're happy, I'm happy for you. But let me let you go. My doorbell just rang, and Jaxson just woke up from his nap."

The two said goodbye, and as soon as she hung up the phone, she picked up Jaxson from his crib before going to get the door. When she opened it, Kareem was standing there in his basketball shorts and a white tee, holding a basketball in his left hand and wearing a smile on his face.

"Hey, you!" Kareem reached to hug Shay with Jaxson in her arms.

"Hey, I thought you weren't going to be around until later," Shay said, looking up at him.

"Yeah, I know. I had to break away from those dudes, especially Donté. He's all in his feelings and shit like a damn girl," Kareem said as he walked inside and sat on the couch. He went on to explain to Shay about Donté.

"Well, y'all been friends for a long time. I guess I'd feel some way if it were me," Shay responded, understanding how Donté felt.

"How was your day? Is your grandmother home?" he asked, changing the subject. The last thing he wanted to do was talk about Donté.

"It was okay—a regular day, quiet. And, no, Ma isn't here. She's at Bible study," Shay answered. Then she went to get Jaxson a snack from the kitchen.

Kareem stayed over Shay's for a while. They watched a couple of movies, took Jaxson outside to sit on the porch, and talked some more. Around six-thirty, Kareem left because his mother would flip if he weren't home for dinner.

Before leaving, he asked her, "How do you feel about meeting my mother and sister?"

Shay stood there for what seemed like forever before answering.

"Sure. Let me know when you want me to come by," she said, smiling while looking at Kareem.

"Cool. I'll see you at the house tomorrow," Kareem said, then hugged her.

It wasn't that Shay didn't want to meet his mother, but she hoped his mother wasn't anything like Ronnie's mother or family period. Like always, Shay was a bit nervous about meeting someone's mother. Meeting Kareem's mother would only give his sister, JaiLynn, more of an opportunity to be nosey and try to be all up in their business.

As soon as Kareem left, Shay's phone rang. She missed the call but didn't recognize the number anyway. Curious to know who was calling her, she called the number back.

"Hello? Someone called me from this number?" she said once the person answered.

"Hey, girl. Long time, no speak. How's my son? I've been trying to call you and shit, but you stopped answering my calls," Ronnie said.

Shay sighed with aggravation.

"What do you want, Ronnie?" she asked, wanting to get the call over with.

"What you think? A nigga's home, and I want to see my son!"

The call was so unexpected. Ronnie was the last person from whom she wanted to receive a call. To add more stress to the stress she already had, she would now have to deal with Ronnie. Shay didn't have the time or energy to dedicate to Ronnie's bull. She thought about just blowing him off, but she only knew it would create bigger problems because he would hunt her down.

"Ughhh!" she said out loud.

*****

Shay couldn't sleep. Tossing and turning, she lay wide awake while thinking about the call from Ronnie. Looking at Jaxson as he slept beside her, she blamed herself for the life he would have while growing up. His father was no good and didn't have his life together; his aunt was crazy and ratchet as hell. Jaxson was still young, but the guilt hung over Shay's head. She had her share in the decision for how Jaxson had come about. Ronnie didn't do it by himself.

After finally falling asleep at two in the morning, Shay was up at six to get ready for school. She woke up to two text messages. One was from Kareem, which put a smile on her face. The other was from Ronnie, which made her regret waking up.

Shay, call me. Stop playing. I'm trying to come see my son. I'm not 'bout to be blowing up your phone. Call me back ASAP.

She sighed. It was much too early for this.

I will call you when I get out of school, Shay texted back.

Kk, he replied.

Shay was on edge all day at school. When she ran into Kareem during fourth period, he sensed something was bothering her.

"You good?" he asked. "Looks like something is bothering you."

"Yeah, I'm good."

"No, you ain't. Wassup? What's on your mind?" Kareem pressed.

Shay liked that he was concerned about what was going on with her. But, truthfully, she wasn't at the point where she wanted to share her baby daddy issues with him. She didn't want him to think she had too much stuff going on and therefore, couldn't be down for him. It was bad enough she had a whole child. Scaring him with baby daddy drama would be too much.

"I'm okay. I don't want to talk about it now, but when I'm ready, I will let you know. Thanks for asking, though," she told him.

"Okay, well, I'm here when you're ready," he said, then reached for her hand and squeezed it gently. "You still coming to the house tonight, right?" Kareem asked.

"Ummm, something came up, and I need to figure some things out. Can we do it another night? I'm so sorry. I want to come, but I can't meet your mother like this. I don't want to give off any bad vibes just meeting your people," she explained.

"It's cool. Take care of whatever you have to take care of, baby girl," he concluded.

19

Ever since that day at the park, Donté had been acting funny. Kareem knew Donté had a hard time adjusting to the fact that he and Eddie had lady friends, but that didn't mean they weren't all boys. Kareem noticed he was moving different— at the games, he didn't ride the bus in the mornings, and he barely made class. It was more than skipping a few days. Donté was noticeably absent.

One day after school, when Kareem was walking from the store, he noticed Donté leaving his house, which was very odd since he didn't visit much. Plus, he hadn't called Kareem to see if he was home. Kareem glanced down at his phone to see if he had missed a call. From a distance, he saw Donté hugging JaiLynn. That made Kareem furious because when it came to his sister, he didn't play. He didn't understand why Donté was at his house in the first place. When Kareem got to the door, he walked in and saw JaiLynn sitting on the couch, smiling as she looked at her phone.

"What's going on? Who was just here?" Kareem asked.

"Donté stopped by," JaiLynn said, looking up at Kareem and then back at her phone.

"Why was he here? What did he want?" Kareem questioned.

"He said he was looking for you, but I don't know. We were talking. Didn't you know he was coming by?" JaiLynn replied.

Kareem looked at his sister before walking towards his room, aggravated. He still couldn't figure out why Donté was at the house and why he didn't call first before coming. He got a strange feeling in his gut and knew he needed to hit up Eddie before he reacted. Sitting at the end of his bed, he pulled out his phone to call Eddie.

"Bro, you talk to Donté today?"

"Nah, why? What happened?" Eddie asked.

"I saw him leaving my house today when I was walking from the store. I didn't know he was coming to my house 'cause he never hit me up, but he was all up on Jai," Kareem explained.

"Say what?" Eddie said, just as shocked as Kareem to hear Donté had been at his house. "Bruh, I don't know what to say, but you gotta find out what's up with that. He's moving funny and acting dumb," Eddie commented.

*****

Later that night, Kareem stayed up talking with Shay. He was still bothered by the fact that Donté came to his house. Shay did admit it was sketchy that he had been there but didn't want to intensify the situation further. So, she gave Donté the benefit of the doubt.

"Maybe you should confront him tomorrow about it in school to see what's up. At least you'll know what's going on and won't be pressed about it," Shay suggested after a few minutes of silence on the phone. "Yeah, you should definitely find out what's going on. You hear me, Kareem?"

"Yeah...my bad, I hear you. I'm gonna do that," Kareem told her. "Enough about that, though. How are you doing? Did you take care of whatever you had to take care of today?" he inquired.

Releasing a big sigh, Shay told Kareem why she was so bothered earlier that day.

"Jaxson's father called me, talking about how he's out and wants to see his son. I was completely thrown off by the call and didn't want to bother you about my issues with my son's father. I don't think I've hated someone so much in my life. But, I don't want to be that girl who keeps her child away from their father because of my dislike for him," Shay explained.

"You know, I never really got it until now. Ain't that some shit. I'm sure my mother went through the same thing when she was dealing with my pops. Dude might not be shit, but don't keep his son away from him. Leave it up to your son to decide whether he wants to have a relationship with his father when he gets older," Kareem told her.

Shay knew Kareem was right, but despite her trying her best to ignore the fact that she was all set with Ronnie, she was madder with herself for dealing with the bullshit with him for so long.

"I hear you," she responded.

"Do you, though?" Kareem asked.

"Yeah, I do."

"Besides, if he's on something where he's trying to slide his way back in...naw, we ain't doing that. Tell ole boy you taken," Kareem stated firmly.

"Man, whatever. We aren't going there," Shay said, grinning.

They both laughed.

"Well, I'm going to let you go. I've kept you up long enough. Baby girl, don't sweat it. Let that man see his son. You're doing your part. He needs to step up and do his," Kareem concluded before hanging up.

20

The next day, Kareem was still pressed over the fact that he needed to speak with Donté. He hadn't seen him. He wasn't on the bus, and no surprise, he wasn't at school either. *What's going on with this dude?* Kareem tried his best to hide his frustration, especially when he saw Shay and Renee walking down the hall.

Looking at Shay was like a breath of fresh air. Blushing, she greeted him and gave him a light hug.

"How are you feeling?" she whispered in his ear. That small gesture put a smile on his face.

"Much better now after seeing you," he replied as they hugged each other again.

"I'll see you after school, okay? Try to have a good day," Shay told him, then continued walking to her next period class with Renee.

While walking to his third-period class, Kareem ran into Eddie, grabbing his books from his locker.

"Wassup, man? What's going on with you? You see that fool Donté yet?" Eddie asked, dapping up Kareem.

"Nah, dawg, I haven't seen him at all. I'm trying not to bug over it. I'm sure there's a reason why he's moving the way he is, and I'll get to the bottom of it."

"Yo, hold up. Let me see something real quick," Eddie said, then pulled out his phone and texted *WYA* to Donté's phone.

Eddie and Kareem waited to see if Donté would reply. It took only two seconds before the indicator in the text messaging app alerted them that the sender was typing a response. The longer they waited for the message to come through, the harder it took for Kareem to remain calm. Eddie looked at Kareem, who stood there looking pissed.

"Yo, what the fuck is really good?" Kareem demanded to know.

Finally, Donté's reply came through. *WHAT'S GOOD, MY G? WASSUP?*

"Wassup? Are you kidding me? That's all he has to say?" Kareem yelled. "Yo, E, call his phone. I don't have time for this. I have questions, and this dude is gonna answer them all."

Eddie dialed Donté's number, but before the phone rang for the second time, Kareem snatched Eddie's phone out of his hand.

"Wassup, yo?" Donté said when he answered.

"Yo, this ain't Eddie. What's going on, my dude? We got drama or something? You coming to my house and stuff without me knowing, hugging all on my sister, and then have the nerve not to answer your phone. Dawg, you acting like you got something to prove. Let me know what's up."

Eddie looked at Kareem and could see the anger that glazed his face. He knew Kareem wasn't to be dealt with, especially when he was hot like that. He couldn't hear Donté on the other end, but he knew Donté didn't want it either.

"Wassup, dawg? You want to let me know what the hell you're thinking?" Kareem asked.

"Man, it isn't...I mean, it wasn't even like that. I don't know what I was thinking. All I know is that I feel like I'm losing my boys to females. So, I thought I could make you feel how I was feeling by linking up with Jai," Donté admitted.

"Yo, what is he saying, bro? Put the phone on speaker," Eddie whispered to Kareem, trying to be nosey. "Press the damn button on the side, dawg," he said, motioning to Kareem.

"Are you serious? That's the stupidest thing I've ever heard. You talking to Jai wasn't going to make me feel the same way you're feeling. That was only going to get you hurt. You bugging," Kareem stated firmly to Donté.

The phone went silent.

"Man, you gonna have to call my sister and end whatever you think you was going to start on my behalf. That ain't the way to go. I gotta holla at you later. You on some crazy shit for real, D!" Kareem said, then hung up the phone, furious and confused. "Dawg!" Kareem said to Eddie while shaking his head.

Eddie burst out laughing. "I know you're pissed, man, and my bad for laughing, but that was the dumbest thing I've heard in a long time. Something else is going on 'cause that doesn't even sound like D," he said.

"I don't know, man, but I'll holla at you after school. That messed me up. He's bugging," Kareem told Eddie, then headed to class.

21

As usual, Shay called Kareem later that evening. She wanted to check on him because she knew he was still pretty upset about what was going on with Donté.

"Hey, what you doing?" she asked.

"Nothing much. Just chillin'. What you doing?" he asked.

"Same stuff, different day. I need a few days away or something," Shay wearily responded.

"That doesn't sound like a bad idea. We should try to plan something. Not nothing big or anything. Something light. Don't we have vacation coming up?"

Kareem and Shay sat on the phone trying to make plans. Nothing that would cost them a lot of money, but something fun where they could bring Jaxson along. Shay appreciated Kareem for thinking to include Jaxson on their weekend trip. It was his idea. Shay wasn't from the area at all, and she most definitely wasn't familiar with anything in Richmond.

"Ummm, I don't know where we should go," she told him. "Unless you're tryin' to go where I'm from, this planning is all you."

"You know what, let's do that. Let me see how you are in your comfort zone around your people," Kareem told her.

"I would love to go see my sister and even my mom. Jaxson hasn't seen her in some time. Last time I was there, they really didn't have a chance to bond. But, I don't want to run into anyone, especially my son's father's people," Shay said.

"Don't worry about none of that. Let's go for a few days, see your people, and enjoy ourselves. I'm not taking no for an answer. You should be seeing your sister more anyway. I can't stand mine, but truthfully, I can't go more than three days without seeing her. She's irritating and all, but that's my little sis, ya know."

*****

A few weeks after Shay and Kareem discussed their plans, they hit the road, taking the three-hour bus ride from Baltimore to

Shay's hometown. They planned on staying at Shay's mother's house. Surprisingly, Shay's mother was open to Shay and the baby staying for the weekend, and she wasn't too bothered when Shay explained she was bringing a very good friend with her so he could see the town. She was very shocked at her mother's openness to Kareem. Ma told Shay how her mother called her and asked if Kareem was a good boy, and if he could be trusted around her daughter and grandson. Most importantly, she wanted to make sure Kareem wasn't like Ronnie. When Ma gave Shay's mother the rundown on how respectful Kareem had been, her mother couldn't have been happier. Moreover, Jaylah, Shay's sister, took a liking to Kareem.

Back home, Shay took Kareem on a tour of the town, taking him to the harbor, the mall, and even the zoo. They all seemed to like the zoo, especially Jaxson. Two days passed since they were in town, and everything seemed to be going well until Sunday evening. They were all chilling at the house when Shay got a text, which read:

So we being cute now? You come to my city with my kid and another dude, and I still haven't seen my son, Shayla? Y'all laughing and looking cute, but the joke is 'bout to be on you.

Shay stared at her phone before taking a deep breath. She felt her heart in her throat. This was what she feared. She knew Ronnie would find out she was in town. *Y'all laughing and looking cute.* She must have looked at those words at least ten times, taking them to mean Ronnie was watching them. Shay couldn't shake the feeling she had, and she hoped Kareem wouldn't see the uneasiness on her face. The last thing she wanted him to do was worry, especially about a dude he didn't know. Then again, Ronnie was unpredictable and capable of doing anything, so maybe Kareem did have something to worry about.

22

Kareem was enjoying being away from Richmond. For him, the trip was bringing him and Shay closer. The comfort she exuded in her hometown was something different for Kareem to see compared to when they were back in Richmond. She smiled more, and he knew the love she had for her sister was the same that he had for JaiLynn. He knew she needed this time with her family, despite whatever issues she had with her son's father. Frankly, Kareem wasn't worried about Ronnie. He'd been so unbothered that he never even asked his name.

"We got two more days here. What you tryin' to do for the remainder of our time?" Kareem asked Shay while they sat on her mother's back porch.

Silence filled the air instead of a response. Kareem looked up at Shay, who appeared to have something on her mind.

"Shay, you hear me? You okay?"

She instantly cleared her throat. "Yeah, I'm sorry. I heard you. Ummm, I don't know. You want to go to DC for the day? That's something we can do," Shay suggested, trying to put Ronnie's text out of her mind, although she was finding it difficult to do.

"I haven't been on a tour of DC in a few years. I heard they built a new museum. That would be something to see," Kareem replied.

Shay was happy Kareem agreed to the plan. Maybe getting away from her house and going into the city would make Ronnie believe they left town. Ronnie was a very angry young man who recently got out of jail, and not knowing what he was capable of doing, Shay was worried about his next move. She didn't find it necessary to take Jaxson to see him, especially since he had nothing to offer him. It certainly wasn't going to happen with Kareem there. It just wasn't the right time or place. But, she couldn't let it go at that, so she told Kareem about the text. He had a right to know what was going on in Ronnie's head.

"You know I'm not scared of him, right?" Kareem told her.

"I never said you were. He's just a lot to deal with. I never met anyone so selfish," Shay replied.

Kareem looked at her. He wanted to be sensitive to what she was going through.

"Okay, don't trip. We're gonna make the best of the next couple of days. I want you to be happy, and I most certainly want you to enjoy yourself. It was the whole point of this trip," he said, reaching to play with a strand of her hair.

Shay sat on the porch, looking at Kareem. She knew everything he was saying was right. She needed to get Ronnie out of her head, but she had a sinking feeling that something wasn't right. Honestly, she was ready for the trip to be over so they could get out of there.

This girl got some nerve bringing another dude to my town. How does she think that shit gon' work out? What she thought, I was just going to sit back and be quiet, knowing I haven't seen my son in what feels like forever? And she got my son out here gallivanting with someone else, Ronnie thought.

Ronnie was far from perfect, but he was trying to do the right thing by his son. A part of him knew he messed up with Shay, but he wanted to fix it. He wanted her. More than that, he wanted to see his son. But how could he make things right? How could he get her to listen to what he had to say, especially with Kareem around?

"Yo, fam, you good?" Ronnie's boy asked him, trying to pass him the joint that they had been circling for fifteen minutes.

"Yeah, fam, I'm good. I'm about to get outta here. I have to deal with some things and figure some stuff out," Ronnie told him. "I'll holla at y'all later."

I'm going to put hands on that dude. If I have to go through him to get to Shay, then so be it, Ronnie thought as he walked down the street.

High from the joint he had just smoked, he was in a trance. A part of him knew he was thinking crazy, but it is what it is.

"I'm going to see him before he thinks he's leaving town," Ronnie said out loud while walking into the liquor store. He was on a whole new level now.

"Baby girl, you ready?" Kareem called out to Shay as he sat in her mother's living room holding Jaxson.

"Yeah, give me one sec," she replied.

"Y'all make sure you have a good time, Kareem. Shay is stressed out. I heard what happened, and I don't want her worrying about that ol' crazy boy, Ronnie," Shay's mother said while sitting on the couch.

"We will," Kareem told her.

Shay, Kareem, and Jaxson walked to the railway station that was down the street from the house. During the two-hour train ride to DC, Jaxson enjoyed looking out the window, pointing when he saw something interesting. Kareem tried his best to show Shay a good time, knowing she was letting Ronnie consume her thoughts.

"Listen, I want you to enjoy yourself, Shay," Kareem said.

"I am having a good time with you," she replied, smiling as she reached for his hand.

It was time to change the conversation. She refused to let Ronnie be the focus of their weekend.

Shay looked at Kareem, who was genuinely concerned about her feelings. She then looked at Jaxson, who was smiling as he looked out the window at the farmers working and the country farms that housed the horses. Shay smiled at the sight of seeing her son smile.

Kareem pulled Shay close to him and kissed her on the forehead, making her feel secure. She loved it when he showed her affection. He always gave her what she needed; he was like a much-needed hug out of nowhere.

"We are almost there, guys. Jaxson, are you excited?" Kareem said as he tickled Jaxson.

After a few stops at different stations, Kareem could see Shay had started to relax and enjoy the day.

"Okay, I'm ready, guys. Let's have a good time!" she said excitedly.

"See, that's what I like to hear. Let's go!"

Once they got into DC, they had to walk about a block before they were at the White House. Once at the White House, they had to walk another block to the bus stop designated for city tours. They took a detour along the way and got Jaxson some ice cream. It was scorching, and there were many people in the area. They stayed close to one another to avoid getting lost in the crowd.

They enjoyed the tour of the Martin Luther King monument, the beautiful view of the cherry blossoms, and the George Washington monument. Overall, it turned out to be an enjoyable day for everybody. They saw some new things and even went to some of the new museums. Shay was shocked to learn that Kareem enjoyed many of the same things she did, which only made the attraction between them stronger.

On the train going back to Baltimore, Shay received a text from Renee, who was checking to see how her weekend was going. Shay kept the text brief, but she let Renee know she would fill her in on everything about Ronnie, her mother, and how Kareem had been so supportive once she got back home.

Make sure you hit me when you get back in town, girl, was the last text Shay read from Renee before turning her attention back to the boys.

25

Shay and Kareem sat in the living room on the couch. It was the day they were to leave to go back home. Shay was relieved that she took the trip because she had the opportunity to build a better relationship with her mother that had always been rocky throughout the years. It was different for them this time around. Shay didn't know if it was because she had raised Jaxson by herself and not succumbed to the pressure, or maybe it was because they had spent enough time apart. Shay was also happy she got the chance to spend time with Kareem, despite the crap Ronnie tried to pull.

Everyone sat talking in the living room before the bus ride home. As usual, Shay was sad about leaving her sister. She hated that Jaylah wasn't around to be with Jaxson. Jaylah loved him, and he was starting to love her, too.

Shay's phone rang; it was Ma calling.

"Hey, Ma," she answered.

"Hey, baby. How was y'all weekend? Did you enjoy it?" Ma asked.

"It was good, Ma, but there's always something. Nothing ever goes as planned," Shay said uneasily.

"Well, you can tell me what happened later. I was just checking on you. Make sure to call me when you get on the bus and let me know when y'all are going to arrive so I can be at the station," Ma concluded.

"Okay, Ma. Love you," Shay told her.

"Love you, too!"

In the living room, everyone's attention was glued to the television screen. The news anchor reported a homicide had just happened at the corner of Lenox and Ashton. Two black males were standing outside of a convenience store in what appeared to be a robbery gone wrong. The room was quiet; no one said anything.

"When stuff like this starts to happen, it's time to go. I'm glad we're leaving today. That's crazy," Shay commented, breaking the silence.

Dannnnnnng, Kareem thought to himself.

The time came for them to head to the bus station, and Shay was relieved. There was nothing she wanted more than to be at home in her own space with her son. She wanted Ronnie to be out of her life so badly, but she knew that wasn't going to happen no time soon. She knew he would make true on his promise to see his son. A part of her felt like she could scare him off by threatening to take him to court, but what would she say? *My son's father has been popping up and trying to contact me to see his son.* She knew she would get shut down because Ronnie presented no real threat. These were the thoughts running through her mind as she sat on the bus going back home. Jaxson and Kareem slept most of the way; Shay stayed awake and stared out the window.

During the ride, she decided to hit up Renee to put her on to all the good things they had done on their trip. But, when she pulled her cell phone out from her bag, she saw that she had another text from Ronnie.

So you really gonna leave town without me seeing my son, Shay? That's what we doing, huh? I guess I'm going to have to come see him. Check for me!

After reading that message, Shay's heart started racing, and her palms instantly got sweaty. She looked over at Kareem, who was peacefully sleeping. She hated to wake him up and bother him with her and Ronnie's issues, but she was scared. She was scared because there were no limits to an angry man who felt like he was being kept from his kid.

Sitting in silence, Shay glanced at Jaxson, who lay next to Kareem. She then looked out the window, caught up in her thoughts. Shay held off on texting Renee; she would talk to her once she got home.

Kareem enjoyed their trip, but he noticed Shay had seemed upset about something once they got home. He asked her several times if anything was wrong, but each time, she told him it was nothing. Not believing her, Kareem told her to call if she needed to talk, and then he headed home.

"Hey, Reem. How was your trip?" his mother asked as she sat in the kitchen preparing dinner.

"It was good, Ma. I really enjoyed myself," he replied.

"So, are you still gonna sit here and tell me she isn't your girlfriend after all this time y'all have been spending together? You seem happy, Kareem, and despite her having a son, I'm going to tell you to be careful," Torrie said with concern.

"Huh? Why you say that?" he asked.

"Son, I'm already hip to the game. Being with your father was quite an experience for me. I'm sure whoever her son's father is, he isn't happy with her moving on to be with another man. They never are. Your father is still on my back, and how many years has it been? Jealousy and selfishness, mixed with pride, will cause a man to do some stupid things. You just watch yourself," she explained.

Kareem sat at the kitchen table thinking about what his mother said. *Damn.* At that moment, he realized the situation could be bigger than what he thought. Ronnie could be crazy enough to do something stupid, and that's the reason he worried about Shay.

Kareem thought about calling her, but then decided he would give her time to relax and call her later. The following day was a holiday, and they didn't have school. So, he planned to sleep in and then maybe hit the park to shoot some hoops.

*****

The next day, Kareem hit up Eddie to see what he was doing.

"Yo!"

"Wassup, man? When you get back?" Eddie asked.

"We got back last night," Kareem explained.

"Cool, cool. I'm glad you're back, 'cause I'm tryin' to shoot some hoops," Eddie told him.

"Bro, bet. Me, too. I'll meet you there in about forty minutes," said Kareem.

"Bet. I'll see you then," Eddie said, ending the call.

As Kareem headed to the kitchen to make himself a bowl of cereal, he came across JaiLynn in the living room watching TV.

"I see you're up early. It would be nice if you got up just as early on a school day," she commented sarcastically.

"I see you got jokes, dummy," he spat back, then playfully jumped at her as he walked by.

Kareem poured his cereal while watching TV from the kitchen. It grew quiet, but he knew how to break the ice.

"I hope you haven't been talking to Donté while I was gone, and I'm not playing."

JaiLynn looked at him and rolled her eyes. Kareem knew his sister knew better. At least he hoped she did. He watched his sister get up from the couch and walk towards her room. She nudged him as she walked by.

"I hope you and him know better, JaiLynn," he snapped, but she never responded.

After eating his cereal, Kareem sat at the table thinking about Shay. He wanted to call her but didn't want to crowd her. After all, they had just spent the weekend together. Instead, Kareem walked to the park, where he saw Eddie off in the distance shooting the basketball in the hoop.

"Man, you still weak!" Kareem yelled.

Eddie turned around with a big grin on his face. "You a hater, bro. You always got something to say."

They both laughed.

Kareem and Eddie were the only people in the park. Kareem shared his weekend with Eddie, telling him what a good time he had with Shay. Eddie informed Kareem what had been going on in town while he was gone. Eddie was still rocking out with Renee, which made Kareem happy. Eddie also told Kareem that he hardly saw Donté and didn't know if he was still trying to talk to JaiLynn.

"Dawg, something ain't right. We have to try to hook up with him and find out what's up. Since when has he ever moved like this? This is our brother, man. We got to find out what he's dealing with."

What Eddie said stayed on Kareem's mind all day. Usually, when he dealt with issues like this, it was natural for him to call Shay so he could vent to her and get her opinion on it. But, he already knew what she would say about this. He knew he had to contact Donté sooner or later to find out what was going on with him.

Walking home, Kareem decided he would call Shay. Not talking to her all day felt more like a week. He wanted to head over to her house but didn't want to seem like he was all on her despite him being. The feelings he felt for Shay were out of this world. Kareem was starting to recognize the emotions he had for Shay would be called love. He had fallen hard for her and was confused about what he should do regarding his new feelings for her. He knew what it was like loving his mother and even JaiLynn, but the thought of loving Shay was something different. Just as he was about to hit send to call Shay, he received a call from his mother.

"Hey, wassup, Ma?" he answered.

"Hey, are you going to be home when I get off work?" she asked.

"Yeah, Ma. Is everything okay?"

"Yes, everything is fine. I just want to see my son when I get home and not have to call and tell you to come home from Shay's house."

"Mannnnn, Ma, you tripping!"

They both laughed and hung up. Then, with the biggest smile, he called Shay.

"Hey, girl, what are you doing?" he asked.

"Nothing much really. Just chillin' in the house," Shay replied, grinning.

"How's Jax?" Kareem asked.

"He's good. He's in the living room with Ma. Probably playing and driving her crazy. Hey…I really appreciate you going home with me. Besides the little crazy things that popped up, I enjoyed my time with you," Shay expressed.

She wanted him to know that it wasn't just a "trip home" for her. Kareem was showing her what she deserved— something Ronnie never cared to do.

"My pleasure," he responded.

Before Kareem could get another word out, there was a loud banging on the door.

"Shay, hold on one sec. Some dummy is knocking at the door like they're the police."

"Police! Open up!

What the fuck! he thought to himself. "Shay, it's the police," Kareem said into the phone.

He was scared. He'd seen too many news segments to believe he couldn't become a statistic. Kareem wasn't sure what to do.

"What?!" Shay was just as surprised as Kareem.

"Hold on. Don't hang up the phone," he told her, then cracked open the door. "Yes, officers?" he said, looking around at all the officers standing at his front door.

Kareem remembered the things his mother had told him regarding how to interact when confronted by the police, stressing that Kareem's job was to get back home safe.

"Kareem Cox?" one of the officers asked, looking Kareem up and down.

"Yes? What's the problem, sir?" he asked, recalling his mother's advice to be respectful and not confrontational.

"You are wanted for questioning at the police station. You need to come with us."

"For what?" he demanded to know.

"We just need you to come with us to the station."

Kareem stood there confused and afraid as the officers placed handcuffs on him. His phone dropped to the floor.

"Shay, call my mama. I don't know what's going on," Kareem said loud enough for her to hear as he was being escorted out his front door.

"Kareem! Kareem! You there?" Shay yelled from the other end of the phone.

Before her line went dead, she heard Kareem say, "Sir, can you tell me what all of this is about?"

27

Shay instantly got a pain in the pit of her stomach. She didn't know what was going on, but she knew it was bad. Since she didn't have his mother's cell phone number, and not wanting to get JaiLynn all upset by calling her, Shay called the hospital and asked to speak to Nurse Torrie.

"This is Torrie. How may I help you?" Kareem's mother said into the receiver.

"Hi, Ms. Torrie. This is Shay. Sorry to call you at work, but I was just on the phone with Kareem, and the police came to the door and took him to the police station. He asked me to call you. I didn't want to call JaiLynn, and the only way I knew to get in contact with you was at the hospital," Shay rambled nervously.

"What?! Shay, baby, slow down for me. Tell me again what's going on," Torrie said, trying not to panic.

Shay took a deep breath and slowly told Kareem's mother what happened. It wasn't long before Torrie showed up at Shay's house to go to the police station and find out why Kareem was taken there.

Once at the police station, officers told Torrie that they needed to question her son about two homicides that happened in Baltimore a few days earlier. Torrie knew her son and Shay were just there a few days ago visiting Shay's family. But, she also knew damn well that her son was not capable of killing anyone, let alone two people.

"Sir, there's been some mistake," she said.

Once Shay heard the reason for Kareem being questioned, her heart sank. She instantly felt sick and ran to the nearby restroom. In her head, she had to wonder if this was what Ronnie meant with his threats. Shay knew he was crazy, but she didn't think he could pull off something so malicious and then try to involve someone who had nothing to do with their mess. She wanted to throw up. Her stomach ached, and her head started to hurt.

"This is all my fault," she cried out.

She must have been in the bathroom for some time, because Torrie came looking for her, full of concern.

"Shay, do you know anything about what they're talking about? Did my son get into some trouble while y'all were in Baltimore?"

Shay looked at Torrie and started crying harder.

"Ms. Torrie, I'm sorry. This is all my fault."

Torrie tried to calm Shay down so she could hear what she was trying to say. She needed to gather all the facts because she knew her son's life would depend on it.

Sobbing on the bathroom floor, Shay explained how Ronnie had made threats against her because she wouldn't let him see his son. She also told Torrie that he grew furious when he learned she came to town and had another guy around Jaxson.

Torrie instantly became angry because she had told her son to be wary of Shay having an ex-boyfriend, but she calmed herself. She didn't have the time it would take to curse out Shay about her baby's daddy. She had to get *her* baby out of jail—whatever that would take.

"Shhh," she said, rubbing Shay's shoulders. "Come on, wipe your face and get it together. We have to be strong for Kareem and figure this out 'cause my son is innocent," Torrie told her.

Angry and confused, Torrie pondered the situation. She hoped her son was okay and prayed he was staying strong.

"Excuse me, sir," Torrie said as she and Shay walked to the front desk. "I need to know what's going on with my son."

Sizing up Torrie and Shay, the officer sitting at the desk replied, "Ma'am, take a seat, and I'll call the detective to come talk to you."

28

The cell was dark. Kareem sat on the bench next to an old cat who looked to be in his forties. He was of average built, wore a dusty hunter green sweater and maroon plaid pants, and smelled like urine. Kareem was pissed that he had to sit in a cell with him until they cleared up this mess.

"What you in here for, man?" the man asked.

Kareem ignored him. The man tapped his hand on the bench, trying to get his attention, and asked again. This time, he slurred his words, his breath smelling like a mix of Ole English and E&J brandy. Kareem coughed and put his fist up to his mouth, trying to keep from inhaling the stench. He had no choice but to answer because he didn't feel like hearing—nor smelling—the man ask him another time.

"I'm here over a misunderstanding, man, and I don't have plans to be here long," Kareem replied.

The guy looked at Kareem and held up his arm as if he was looking at a watch.

"That's what they all say, kid," he said, then profusely coughed until he leaned his head on the metal bars behind him.

Kareem turned his body around and tried to imagine himself being somewhere other than where he was presently. He wondered how he got in this situation. Back in the day, he, Donté, and Eddie would get in minor trouble, but nothing resulted in anything this serious. Kareem stayed away from certain situations that he knew would put him in jail if caught because he didn't want to do that to his mother. She went through enough with his dad, and it took a lot out of her. He didn't want to be the cause of more anguish for her.

Kareem sat there with his head held down in disbelief. He heard the iron door slam and the heavy footsteps of the guard who periodically walked back and forth to check on the inmates. His keys rattled with each step he took, hitting the back of his gun. The sound of his flashlight sliding against the walls irritated Kareem even more as he tried to process his situation.

"Ummm, excuse me, sir. When do you think I can get my call?" Kareem asked.

The officer smirked, then looked down at his watch. Without responding to Kareem, he just kept walking.

"This is your first time in the slammer, kid, isn't it?" the older guy asked.

Ignoring the man's question, Kareem took a deep breath and kicked the metal bars that held him hostage.

The officer went to the back and returned with another guard. They walked towards Kareem's cell and proceeded to unlock the door.

"You got five minutes, kid," the second officer said.

"What?" yelled the old guy.

"Be quiet, Ernest!" one of the cops shouted back.

"You know what, fuck y'all! I'm going to need my call, too," the guy said, then stood up and started adjusting his sweater.

"Have a seat, Ernest. You're in here every other day. Whoever you're calling knows where you are," the other officer said.

Kareem looked back at the old guy as he walked out of the cell.

"Screw y'all," Ernest said, sliding back down on the floor.

The officer walked Kareem to the phone and sat him down at the desk.

"Who you want to call, kid?" he asked.

"My mother, Torrie," Kareem replied.

"What's her number?" the officer asked.

Kareem provided his mother's number to the officer and watched as he dialed.

"Here you go, kid," the officer said, extending the phone's receiver to Kareem.

"Thanks," Kareem said, then sat there anxiously as the phone rang. "Come on, Ma. Pick up," he whispered as the phone continued to ring.

His legs began to shake, and his hands started getting clammy.

"Hello, hello," his mother said, finally answering.

"Ma, it's me. Where are you, Ma? I don't know what's going on," Kareem blurted out, his voice trembling as he struggled not to cry.

"Baby, I'm here. Calm down. Shay called me, and we are both here."

Kareem was relieved to hear they were at the police station.

"Ma, they didn't even tell me what I did. They came to the house talking about they had some questions, and no one asked me anything. This ain't right, man. This is bogus," Kareem further explained.

"What? What you mean you don't know why you're here? They can't do that."

Kareem could tell by his mother's tone that she was pissed.

"Excuse me, officer. You mean to tell me that my minor child is being held, and you didn't tell him what charges he's being held on?" Kareem heard his mother ask an officer. "You have my minor child up here in a jail cell," she continued. "You came to my home and told him that you had some questions to ask him. Yet, you did not call his parent. Y'all got the right one today! He's only seventeen, not eighteen. That means an adult should be present with him, correct?" she yelled, then turned her attention back to Kareem, who was listening on the other end.

"Baby, I don't know what's going on, but these law-breaking cops got the right one. We're going to figure this out. I'm here; I got you. We're going to get to the bottom of this. I'm about to call your uncle Mike because we're about to get an attorney to handle this. I love you, Reem. Hang tight," she said, then hung up.

Before she disconnected the call, Kareem heard his mother still questioning the officers like she was prosecuting them. One would've sworn she had gone to law school or something. Kareem smiled slightly, knowing his mother would get to the bottom of this. He needed all of the energy his mother had just given him to endure whatever was about to happen.

"Kid, do you know why you're here?" the officer asked, overhearing Kareem's conversation.

"Nah. I was told y'all had some questions to ask me, but no one has asked me anything yet. Then, I was placed in a holding cell."

The officer looked at Kareem in such a way that Kareem didn't know if he had said something wrong. The officer no longer gave Kareem eye contact; his eyes stayed glued to the computer. Several seconds later, another officer came and walked Kareem back to the cell.

29

Torrie sat next to Shay in the police station livid and confused. She couldn't believe what was going on. She spent her time pacing back and forth, angrily looking at the officer who sat behind the glass window. Torrie thought she had done everything right by her children. So, she couldn't understand what or who had placed her son in this situation. Thinking about Kareem in a cold, dark cell brought the tears that she had been trying to keep at bay. Torrie quickly wiped them away and pulled herself together.

"Shay, do me a favor. Call and check on Jai for me. I'm going to try to get in contact with my brother," Torrie stated, then stepped outside and dialed Mike's number.

The phone rang several times before he answered.

"Wassup, sis?"

"Mikey," she sobbed.

"What's going on, T?" he asked anxiously. He knew things were serious when Torrie referred to him as Mikey.

"You gotta get down here. They arrested Kareem. They're saying he had something to do with a murder that happened in Baltimore over the weekend. I need you down here," Torrie said, crying.

If anyone could help her sort this mess out, it was Mike.

"I'm already in town. I was going to stop by and see y'all tomorrow. Where are you now?" Mike asked, quickly making his way to his vehicle.

"We're at the police station downtown," Torrie told him, crying harder as she gave in to her fear of something happening to Kareem while he was behind bars.

"I'm on my way, Torrie, but I need you to calm down. We're going to figure this out. Kareem is going to be alright. You hear me?"

Torrie nodded her head before verbally responding to him. Hanging up the phone, she took a deep breath and walked back inside the police station.

"I want you to go home to your baby," she told Shay. "I appreciate you being here and calling me, but you gotta get home.

Can you do me a favor and ask your grandmother if it's okay if JaiLynn comes to your house while my brother and I figure this out? I really need you to do that for me."

"Yes, ma'am," Shay said, tears rolling down her face.

Torrie gave her a big hug.

"We're going to figure this out. Tell your grandmother that I apologize for having you out so long." Torrie reached inside her pocket and handed Shay a twenty-dollar bill. "Take this, go across the street, and catch a cab home."

Shay was reluctant to take the money, but she did as she was told. Torrie stood in front of the police station to make sure Shay was safely in the cab before going back inside the police station. She stopped to get some water from the fountain, taking a few sips to calm herself. She then took some deep breaths, preparing herself to go to battle for her son.

30

Shay sat scared in the back of the cab. She couldn't believe everything that was going on. A part of her felt like it was her fault, but the truth was she couldn't prove Ronnie had done anything. She pulled out her phone and called JaiLynn.

"Hey, Jai. This is Shay. Are you home?" she asked.

"Hey, Shay. Yeah, I'm at home. What's up?" JaiLynn replied.

"I'm coming from downtown. Your brother got arrested, and your mother is at the police station with your uncle Mike. I'm on my way to your house. You need to pack a bag. Your mother wants you to stay at my grandmother's house tonight," Shay explained.

JaiLynn sat quietly on the phone. She had plenty of questions but didn't know what to ask first.

"What are you talking about, Shay? You're scaring me."

"It's too much to talk about on the phone. I'll tell you when I get there. I'll be there in ten minutes."

The cab pulled up to the bricks in front of JaiLynn's house. Shay asked the driver if he wouldn't mind waiting while she went in to get JaiLynn. He agreed to wait and was even kind enough to stop the meter when Shay got out of the cab.

Shay skipped up the stone stairs and rang the bell. After looking out of the second-floor window, JaiLynn buzzed her in. Inside the hall, Shay slowly walked to the door and took a deep breath, preparing for the onslaught of questions JaiLynn would have. Once JaiLynn opened the door, she stood there in tears.

"I've been trying to call my mother, but she ain't answering, Shay. What's going on?" JaiLynn asked.

Shay hugged JaiLynn and felt her body trembling.

"She's at the station, probably talking to the officers or something. She doesn't know how long she's going to be there, so she wants you to come home with me. Come on, get your bag. The cab is waiting. Make sure you grab your school stuff, too. I'll text your mother when we get to my grandmother's house," Shay told her.

JaiLynn grabbed her stuff, and they headed down the stairs. They didn't have to go far, considering Shay lived only a few blocks away from JaiLynn and Kareem. Once in the house, Shay told her grandmother and JaiLynn about the events that occurred earlier with Kareem. After hearing the story, JaiLynn was furious because she knew her brother didn't belong in jail. For what? He didn't do anything. Ma told Shay that she was going to try to call Torrie.

"Something ain't right 'bout all of this, Shay. That's a good boy. He didn't do what they are trying to say he did. God, give that boy the strength to get through this!" Ma prayed while holding Jaxson in her arms as she walked out of the kitchen.

JaiLynn slept in the room with Shay and Jaxson. Shay spent most of the night fidgeting with her phone. Before she went to bed, Shay texted Torrie and told her that JaiLynn was with her at her house. Shay received a text back asking if JaiLynn was sleep. A few moments later, JaiLynn's phone rang. It was Torrie.

"Hey, baby, I know you're worried, and I'm sure Shay told you what's going on. But, Uncle Mike and I are here trying to figure things out. I don't want you to worry. I will be home when you get home from school tomorrow. Hopefully, Reem will be, too. Don't mention anything to anyone, okay? I will take care of everything," Torrie assured her.

"Yeah, Ma, I hear you. Keep me posted, and tell Reem I love him," JaiLynn said before hanging up and turning over to go to sleep.

Shay was sure all JaiLynn needed was to hear her mother reassure her that everything was going to be alright.

Shay lay in bed looking at Jaxson, who was sound asleep in his crib. She couldn't sleep; she had too much on her mind. She wanted to talk to Kareem and hear his voice. She had gotten so used to talking to him every night that it didn't feel normal not to speak to him before she went to bed. Her personal space felt cold. It bothered her what was happening. Furthermore, she knew everything about the situation was not right.

31

Kareem sat in the cell for about three hours before the detectives brought him in for questioning. An average-built, well-dressed, stocky detective walked in the room. He was somewhat intimidating, but Kareem wasn't bothered by him. He was too angry and focused on the reason he was there to be intimidated.

"Kid, since you're under the age of eighteen, we can't question you without an adult present. My partner informed me that your mother and uncle are in the front lobby. Your uncle can't come in, but we can bring your mother back to sit with you. You can deny it, but this is your right. Are you cool with this, young brother?" the officer asked.

Kareem agreed for his mother to come and sit with him. He felt relieved seeing here. As soon as she entered the room, he embraced her like he hadn't seen her in a lifetime.

"You alright, baby?" Torrie asked, stepping back to get a good look at him.

"Yeah, I'm alright. I'm so glad to see you," Kareem confessed.

He was physically a man, but on the inside, he was still that little six-year-old boy who had fallen and scraped his knee, running into Torrie's arms for her to make it better.

"Mama, I don't know what's going on. I promise you that I didn't do anything. This is crazy, Ma," he said, pleading his case and hoping she believed him.

"I know, I know. Something isn't right about this, but we're going to get to the bottom of it. Don't say anything because we don't have a lawyer here yet. Uncle Mike has called one, though," Torrie told him.

Torrie and Kareem sat next to each other while another detective came into the room.

Before the second detective could sit down, Torrie asked, "Is it lawful to bring a minor in for questioning and have him detained in a cell for an outrageous amount of time without informing him why he has been arrested?"

The room went silent. Before the detectives could proceed with any questions, Torrie informed them that they would have to wait a bit longer until their lawyer arrived. Torrie could tell by the detectives' expressions that they were aggravated.

"Y'all got the right one this time. What y'all did to my son was wrong!"

Pushing out of their seats, the detectives told Torrie and Kareem that they would be back once they got word that their attorney had arrived. Kareem was okay with that since his mother was present.

"Ma, this is wild. This can't be legal," he stated.

"It's not, and we're going to get to the bottom of this. I promise you that," Torri replied.

Torrie and Kareem sat quietly in the room for what seemed like hours. An hour passed before Kareem's attorney arrived. He looked to be in his mid-forties, had tight swag, and was articulate. He entered the room like he meant business. Behind him walked in the two detectives. Kareem's attorney turned to ask the detectives could he have a minute to confer with his client. The detectives said nothing and left the room.

The detectives allowed the attorney ten minutes to speak with Kareem before they returned to the room. After the attorney introduced himself to the detectives as Jason Whitley, the detectives began asking Kareem questions about the murders.

"Mr. Cox, were you in the DC area around April 21st?"

Kareem looked at his attorney, waiting for a signal to respond.

"You may answer," his attorney told him.

"Yes," Kareem replied.

"What was your reason for being in that area on that date?" the first detective questioned.

Kareem looked at his attorney again for permission to speak before replying, "I was with my girlfriend visiting her family."

"Do you know an individual by the name of Charles Oakley?"

Kareem looked at his attorney and then at his mother. "No. Who is that?"

Before the detectives had a chance to continue with their questioning, Kareem's attorney intervened.

"Is my client being charged with a crime here, brothers? Please help me understand why you are questioning him?" Mr. Whitely asked.

One of the detectives stated that Kareem was brought into questioning because someone identified him as a primary suspect in Charles Oakley's homicide. Kareem's mouth dropped when he heard what he was being accused of.

"The devil is a damn lie!" Torrie shouted in anger. "Not my child! You got the wrong one!"

Kareem was in a state of shock, and it felt like the walls were starting to close in around him. His face and forehead flushed with heat as he grew angrier. He wanted to speak but choked on his words. Not wanting to appear weak in front of the detectives, he wiped at the tears that lined his eyes.

"What?! I didn't kill nobody. This is some type of mistake."

"I heard you say that he was identified as being present in the area where this man was killed. Is that correct?" Mr. Whitely asked for clarity.

"Yes, sir," the second detective responded.

"Again, I ask, is my client being arrested and charged with a crime? He has already been held illegally. You know that, right?" Mr. Whitley stated while noting something on his writing pad.

Torrie listened intently to Mr. Whitley, hoping his statement would get Kareem off the hook for something she knew her son had not done.

"Well, no, we don't have anything to charge this young man with, but we are working to find out what's going on. This is an ongoing investigation. Since Mr. Cox doesn't have a record, we're going to let him go. However, this is a very serious matter involving a man being murdered, so we may need to call him back in for questioning."

The second detective looked Kareem in his eyes while explaining to him that pending the investigation, he couldn't leave the state of Virginia until informed otherwise.

Before concluding their questioning, the first detective asked, "Kid, if you're not from the Baltimore area, do you have any idea who would specifically identify you as a suspect to this crime?"

Overwhelmed, Kareem dropped his head. Then he looked up at his mother, whose eyes were bloodshot red. As his attorney continued to jot down notes, Kareem instantly thought of Ronnie, Jaxson's father. At that moment, it hit him that he had been set up. He slowly turned his head to look the detective in his eyes.

"No, sir, I don't."

32

Torrie was hurt that her son was being accused of doing such a thing, and her heart ached every time she looked at Kareem. He didn't deserve this. Torrie was limited as to what she could do besides continue to advocate for him. She looked over at her son, who was tired, and just wanted to take him home. Torrie then looked over at Mr. Whitely, who was jotting notes in his notebook. She was relieved that her son would get to go home, but he was still going to be dealing with this issue until his name was cleared.

The detectives made it very clear to Torrie and Kareem that it was important for Kareem not to get into any more trouble.

"Sir, I understand the severity of this case," Torrie responded sharply. "My son is not a delinquent, and besides him living in a society where he is judged because of his skin color, he knows what is right and what is wrong. He wasn't in any trouble to begin with. You people are the ones who are trying to pin a crime on him that he didn't commit. I raised him better than that."

Without responding to Torrie, the detectives escorted her and Mr. Whitely to the front lobby. They informed them that they would bring Kareem to them as soon as he was processed out. After an hour, Kareem was led to the front lobby. Hugging her son tightly, Torrie told him that they were going to get through this.

Torrie knew her son was drained. It was after midnight, and Kareem was experiencing one of the worst times of his life. Once they got home, she would make sure he got something hot to eat and went straight to bed. She told him that he could stay home from school the next day if he wanted.

"Mike, I'm going to take him home," Torrie told her brother, who was talking to Mr. Whitley on the sidewalk in front of the police station.

"I'll be right behind you, T," he replied.

Before leaving the police station, Torrie called JaiLynn, but she didn't answer the phone. Figuring JaiLynn had already gone to sleep, she called Shay.

"Hey, Ms. Torrie, is everything okay?" Shay asked, sitting up quickly in the bed.

"Kareem is with me, and we're leaving the police station. Everything is just getting started, but we're going to get to the bottom of this. Thanks for going to get JaiLynn for me. In the morning, please have her call me before y'all go to school. And please tell your grandmother I got her message and appreciate her prayers," Torrie expressed, trying to stifle a yawn.

Kareem was quiet the whole ride to the house,

"Tell me how you're feeling, son," Torrie said.

"Ma, I don't know how some shit like this could happen. I'm tight. What those detectives are trying to say I did is bull. What do I look like committing a crime like that? I'll fight before anything. Plus, who the hell is the man that they suspect I killed?" Kareem responded.

Normally, Torrie would have chastised Kareem for using profanity in front of her, but he had earned the right to say what he needed to.

33

The first thing Kareem did when he got home was take a long, hot shower, and he stayed in there forever. The stench of Ernest was all over him—the smell of buzz and urine permeating his pores. He never felt so dirty in his life.

While getting out of the shower, he heard his uncle and mother talking in the kitchen. As soon as he got dressed, he headed toward the kitchen to join them.

"You feeling better, man?" Mike asked with deep concern.

"I'm alright, Unc. I just can't believe any of this. Everything they did was wrong. Unc, I've never felt so violated in my life. On top of that, who is that man? I have never heard of him," Kareem explained.

"My lawyer is going to deal with that legal stuff 'cause those officers were dead wrong. Once my lawyer is done with them, they better hope they just end up on administrative leave and not terminated. But what happened, nephew? Help me understand this thing," Mike replied.

There was little for Kareem to explain. He told his uncle how he went with Shay to see her family in Baltimore. He explained that the trip was decent; they had a good time and hadn't run into any real drama. However, he did share that some little things had happened. His uncle pressed him to explain what he meant by "real drama".

"Baby, something isn't right. How was Shay acting? Was she off?" Torrie asked. "You got to pay attention to the signs," she continued before he could answer. "The girl told me that Jaxson's father was threatening her because she wouldn't let him see the baby, and he was even more upset because she came there with you."

Once Torrie told Kareem what Shay had told her, it hit him. There were times during the trip that Shay seemed to be preoccupied. Every time he asked her what was up, she told him everything was fine. Kareem instantly thought about what kind of threats Jaxson's father could have been sending her. He sat in deep thought; it was like he blacked out. For a moment, he didn't hear anything his mother and uncle were saying. Suddenly, he remembered the breaking news report they had seen on TV before he and Shay left Baltimore. He hadn't put two and two together, but it was all starting to make sense now. Quickly, he snapped out of it.

"I got to call Shay to see if she knew that Jaxson's father was going to set me up," Kareem said, aggravated.

"I know you're upset, nephew, but take it easy on her because you don't know what she's gotta say. Hear her out. I would hope she wouldn't put you in a situation like that. T, do these young girls do that type of stuff?" Mike asked.

Not waiting around to hear his mother's response, Kareem stormed out of the kitchen and went to his room, shutting the door behind him. He didn't want his uncle and mother to be in his business. That didn't stop them from ear hustling from the kitchen, though.

The phone rang, and Shay answered the phone wide awake.

"Hello, hello...Kareem, is that you?" she asked, confused.

"Yeah, it's me. I just got home not too long ago. Is my sister sleep?" he asked.

Before Shay could reply, he interrupted her.

"I have a question, and please don't lie to me, Shay," he said firmly.

He wanted nothing less than the truth from her.

Again, before she could answer, he asked, "Did you know Jaxson's father was going to try to set me up?"

"No, I didn't," she answered, then began to weep. "Kareem, I didn't know he was going to do something like this. He was upset and kept threatening me because I wouldn't let him see Jaxson, telling me that he was going to find a way to see my son. I promise I didn't know anything about that stunt he pulled, and I am sorry," Shay said, pleading her case.

She cried because she felt guilty about what Kareem was going through. She felt if she had told Kareem what was going on, they might have been able to avoid all of this. She further explained that she didn't tell Kareem about the threats because she didn't want to get him involved with her baby father's drama. She told

him that it was one of the reasons she didn't want to go back —
because Ronnie was out, and she didn't want to deal with his
drama. But she also didn't want to turn down the trip that Kareem
had been looking forward to them taking together.

There was silence on the phone as they processed the things
that were said.

Kareem knew deep down in his heart that Shay didn't have
anything to do with it. He just needed to hear it from her mouth.
He loved her deeply, but he couldn't tell her now. He needed to
protect his feelings. Kareem didn't know what to do next. In a
way, he felt their relationship was tainted by the actions of an idiot
who he had never met. Someone was going down for this, and he
knew it wasn't going to be him because he didn't do anything.

The silence again was palpable. Kareem couldn't take hearing
Shay cry. So, he ended the call and told her that he would talk to
her the next day.

Kareem lay on his bed, looking up at the ceiling. He was trying
to put himself in Shay's situation and think what he would've
done. But it was hard because he didn't have any kids, and he
didn't take too lightly to threats. He replayed her words over and
over again, trying to make sense of everything. Finally, he rolled
out of bed and walked back to the kitchen, where his uncle and
mother were still talking.

"I didn't want to leave before I knew you were okay," Mike
said when Kareem entered the kitchen.

"You want to talk about it, baby?" his mother asked.

"Not tonight, Ma. I just came to get something to drink. I need
to go to bed," Kareem replied.

Torrie knew her son, and she knew he wanted someone to pay
for this. But at what cost? Would she lose her son over this mess?

34

The following morning, Torrie woke up with a prayer in her heart. She knew she had to cover her son with a blessing. She knew he was angry, and she prayed he wouldn't do something to get himself in more trouble, such as seeking revenge.

"Heavenly Father, I pray that you cover my son during this time. I ask that You keep him focused and humble, as his circumstances could have been much different. God, I pray that You allow him to see that the devil targets the most powerful as a distraction from being great. I know Kareem is strong, courageous, and a God-fearing young man. I ask that You continuously allow him to speak to You. Amen."

Just as Torrie was wrapping up her prayer, her phone rang. It was JaiLynn.

"Ma, are y'all okay? I was so worried. Where's Kareem?" she asked anxiously.

"I know you were worried, and we have a lot to talk about when you get home. Your brother is here with me. I need you to go to school and have a good day, Jai." Then, as an afterthought, she added, "I love you, Jai."

After getting off the phone with JaiLynn, she went to Kareem's room to check on him. She opened the door to his room to find him gone. A part of her started to panic until she went down the hall and saw him already dressed and in the kitchen eating cereal while watching TV.

"How you feeling this morning, Reem?" she asked.

"I'm alright, Ma. Still in a state of shock and still upset, but I prayed on it. I had a bad dream that I did something to that man, and there went my future...gone! Karma ain't nothing to play around with. I have faith that everything will turn out how it should," Kareem told her.

Torrie was shocked. The fact that he prayed on this situation and articulating his thoughts in a manner that she knew he would have caused chaos over made her happy. He trusted that what was done in the dark would come to light. She walked over to Kareem and kissed him on his forehead.

"I got you on this, baby boy. You hear me?" she asked, looking him in the eye.

"Yeah, Ma, I know," Kareem replied, leaning to kiss his mother's cheek.

"You know you don't have to go to school today if you don't want to. I can excuse you today, but you still have some explaining to do about all the other days you think I don't know you've been skipping school," she said with a raised brow.

Stunned that she knew, Kareem looked up at his mother, milk dripping out of his mouth from the cereal he had just shoved down his throat.

They both started laughing.

"Nah, Ma, I'm going to go. Plus, I have to find out what's good with Shay," he told her.

"Okay. Well, check on your sister while you're there. She was worried about you. And wait until after school to talk with Shay about this situation. It's not a matter y'all should focus on while you're there. You don't want to get upset and have people all in your business," Torrie advised.

Kareem continued eating his cereal before he stopped suddenly.

"Ma, can I ask you a question?" he asked.

"Sure. What's up?" Torrie replied.

"If you were Shay, what would you have done?"

At first, Torrie was at a loss for words. She pulled up a chair and sat next to Kareem.

"Son, I'm not sure what I would have done if I were Shay. However, it's easy for me to relate to what she's going through. Dealing with your father wasn't easy, and while there were times he ruined every chance I had to be with someone else, I let him because I was young, dumb, and naïve. Part of me isn't mad with Shay because I know how it feels to be in her situation. Maybe she didn't tell you because she wanted to protect you and didn't want you to get in trouble. Those are my thoughts, and I'm trying to be positive because you're my son. But I can't say what I would have done if I were her. You need to have that conversation with her and find out what she's going to do now, because her son's father is somewhere plotting his next move."

Kareem sat at the table, reflecting on what his mother said. He looked down at his phone to check the time. It was almost time for him to head to the bus. He then looked over at his mother, who was taking her time making her morning coffee.

"Ma, you ain't going to work today?" he asked.

"Yeah, I am. I'm going in a few hours later this morning. I was going to call out, but I wanted to wait and see if you were straight first," she explained.

Kareem watched his mother as she stood next to her Keurig and then walked to the kitchen table, her bed scarf hanging halfway off her head. He thought she must have felt it about to slip off, because she reached up and pulled it completely off. Her long brown hair dropped past her shoulders.

"Alright, Ma. I love you, but I gotta go," Kareem said, putting his bowl in the sink and grabbing his coat next to the door.

Torrie asked God to continue to cover him and rid any negative spirits from her son that wasn't a reflection of God.

35

The following morning, Shay woke up still upset about Kareem. She felt responsible for Ronnie's actions. Many thoughts were running through her head, like how did he know Kareem's name to try to link him to such a crime? Furthermore, Kareem had nothing to do with her decision not to let Ronnie see Jaxson. The more she thought, the more her temples began to throb. She looked at JaiLynn, who was primping in the mirror. Jaxson lay in his crib, quietly looking at JaiLynn as she got ready for school. The sight of her son gave Shay reassurance that she had done the right thing by him. It was her job to protect him.

Shay walked out of her room and into the kitchen, where her grandmother sat drinking her coffee and watching the morning news.

"Good morning, baby. How are you feeling?" she asked.

"Ma, this is too much," Shay replied, then explained everything Kareem told her the previous night.

Ma knew Shay was hurt and conflicted about what to do, but she said something that got her attention.

"Baby, have you put yourself in Kareem's shoes?" Ma asked.

Shay sat there quietly processing what her grandmother said. So caught up in her own feelings, she hadn't taken the time to consider what Kareem was going through and the fact that this could cost him his future.

"Ughhhh!" she emitted out of frustration, then leaned over to kiss her grandmother's cheek. "Thanks, Ma."

Shay excused herself from the table to get ready for school. Before walking back to her room, she got Jaxson's bottle out of the fridge. When she returned to her bedroom, she found JaiLynn sitting at the foot of her bed and talking on the phone.

"Shay, my mother said good morning and thank you to you and your grandmother," JaiLynn said.

"Tell her she's very welcome," Shay replied, then asked, "Jai, can you keep an eye on him while I go to the bathroom and get dressed?" She cooed at Jaxson as he stood in his crib, his attention focused on JaiLynn.

Once out of the bathroom, Shay picked up Jaxson from his crib and threw him up in the air. He was happy with the morning attention from his mother.

"Hey, Mama's baby," Shay said, walking him to the living room where Ma was now sitting.

As Shay handed over Jaxson to her, Ma told Shay that things were going to be alright because God makes no mistakes.

"And I'm going to put Ronnie on my prayer list. He needs to be covered by the blood of Jesus," Ma concluded.

When JaiLynn came out of the room and told Shay it was time to leave, Shay instantly got a pain in the pit of her stomach. She was nervous because she was going to have to face Kareem, and she wasn't sure what to say to him. The last time she saw Kareem was when they got back from their trip. She didn't know if Kareem was going to school, but there was no way to avoid him. She owed him answers to any questions he had.

Shay told Ma that she would be home right after school. Ma turned the channel to Jaxson's morning cartoons, sat him on the floor, and headed to the kitchen to make him a bowl of Cream of Wheat.

After the two girls left out the door to walk to their bus stop, JaiLynn asked Shay if she was okay because she had heard Shay talking to her grandmother about Kareem. Shay told her that she was going to be fine; it was just a lot to take in.

As they hit the corner, JaiLynn saw Kareem and took off running toward him. Shay watched as JaiLynn embraced Kareem, and he hugged her tightly to him. Shay could see there was a lot of love between them. They exchanged words, and Kareem smiled at JaiLynn before playfully mugging her face. JaiLynn swatted at him and then went to talk to her friends.

Shay started walking toward Kareem. The closer she got, the more hesitant she became. Kareem looked at her, showing no indifference towards her. When Shay stopped in front of him, Kareem pulled her to him, hugging her tightly. Shay embraced Kareem long and hard. Part of her wanted to shed tears, but she was happy that he showed her the same love. He whispered in her ear, and Shay nodded as he spoke. Kareem released her, kissing her lips quickly as the school bus approached.

"You heard me?" he asked. "We're going to figure this out."

Walking on the bus, Eddie nudged Kareem.

"What's going on, man?" Eddie asked.

"Bro, we got to talk about some things later," Kareem told him.

Eddie leaned his head closer to Kareem and asked, "Man, is she pregnant?"

"No, stupid," Kareem replied.

They walked to the back of the bus, and there sat Donté, who must have gotten on at a previous stop. Eddie stopped and then looked at Kareem. Kareem looked at Eddie, Shay, and then Donté. The disdain he had for Donté was evident in his eyes. Donté didn't say anything to any of them. Shay was scared that Kareem was going to snap. She hoped he didn't because he already had enough to deal with.

At school, Kareem and Shay didn't discuss the issue. As he told her earlier, they would talk about it later. He didn't want to make things obvious to everyone. But, if anyone knew Shay better than Kareem, it was Renee, and Shay couldn't keep anything from her even if she tried. In the library, Renee rolled up on Shay while she sat at the table studying.

"Girl, I've been trying to get in touch with you since last night, but you didn't answer. Is everything good?" Renee asked.

Shay told Renee to pull up a chair and come close because she didn't want everyone in her business. Besides, the librarian always tripped when she heard the students having entertaining conversations rather than studying. After making Renee promise not to say a word to anyone, including Eddie, Shay whispered to her everything that had gone down with Kareem.

"Now remember, you promised not to say anything to Eddie. Wait until he brings it up to you, because I'm sure Kareem is going to run it to him," Shay pleaded.

"You know I got you, girl," Renee replied, then asked, "So what's next?"

Shay didn't know, and she wasn't sure she would any time soon. She knew she would have to talk with Kareem about it after school. She would also have to confront Ronnie.

Leaving the library, Shay ran into Kareem while he was walking to his fifth-period class.

"You good?" Kareem asked.

"Yeah, I'm cool."

As they were walking in the hall, they both stopped quickly. Coming down the hall was Chris. He was wearing an orange velour sweatsuit and white Reebok sneakers with an orange and light blue FUBU headband. They looked at each other and burst out in laughter.

"Wassup, Chris!" Kareem yelled.

"Wassup, Kareem! Hey, Shay," he replied as he shimmied down the hall.

They didn't want to laugh, but Chris's clothing was always a statement. Chris didn't have quite the swag he thought he did. He had a fashion sense, but he applied it all in the wrong way, making it hard for others to ignore.

"I'm going to come to your house after school, okay?" Kareem told Shay.

They hugged and then headed in different directions to their respective classes.

36

After school, Kareem made sure he walked JaiLynn home before heading to Shay's. He was thinking about having this conversation all day in school, but he knew it wasn't the time or place. He knew having the sit-down was necessary, no matter how much it upset him.

Walking to Shay's door, he paused in the apartment's hallway. He needed a minute to get his thoughts together because he didn't want to flip on her. He thought about the things his mother said to him earlier that morning.

Once at the front door, Kareem pulled out his phone and texted Shay, letting her know he was at the door. It took only a few seconds for her to open the door. Shay had Jaxson in her arms. Kareem smiled. He spent so much time with Jaxson that it made him happy when he saw him. Kareem held out his arms, and Jaxson grinned while reaching for him.

"Is your grandmother home?" Kareem asked as Shay stepped back to let him inside.

"She went to Walmart to pick up some stuff for the house," Shay replied.

"Cool, cool," Kareem said, sitting down on the couch with Jaxson.

Kareem continued to play with Jaxson, but the truth was he didn't know where to begin the conversation.

"Reem, I'm sorry I didn't say anything to you about the threats I was getting from Ronnie. He was talking, but he didn't say anything about doing anything to you. I'm hurt because I care about you…"

Shay grew silent. She didn't know what else to say.

"Say no more. It took me talking to my mother to help me see this from another side. That could have easily been her and my messed-up dad. He was on some 'If I can't be with you, you can't be with anyone else' shit. That's the same thing with Jaxson's father, isn't it? But, that man needs to understand that there are other ways of doing things," Kareem said angrily, then asked, "You talk to him yet?"

Shay told Kareem that she hadn't confronted Ronnie about what she believed he did. If he was the reason behind all of this, she didn't want him to know his plan had worked. As far as Shay knew, he didn't know she had put the pieces of the puzzle together, and she wanted to keep it that way.

At the end of their conversation, they decided Shay would confront Ronnie about trying to implicate Kareem in the Baltimore homicide. Other than calling Kareem's uncle Mike to contact a lawyer to have his name cleared, they didn't know what else to do. Overall, the whole thing sucked for Kareem. He wanted Shay to help him clear his name, but this wasn't a random dude. If Ronnie was found guilty, he could do more time, and he just got out. Kareem instantly thought about Jaxson. He was once in Jaxson's shoes when he was little and his father went to jail. Kareem thought about it and thought about it some more.

At that time, Kareem realized he needed to be selfish and think about himself. After all, this could affect the rest of his life. He apologized to Jaxson, but he mattered first. Not Shay, not Jaxson, and damn sure not Ronnie.

Kareem left Shay's house with a sense of relief. All he wanted was for his name to be cleared in the mess that Ronnie had created for him.

37

Later that night, Shay thought about the things she and Kareem discussed. She regretted ever dealing with Ronnie, but that would've meant she wouldn't have Jaxson, who was the best thing to ever happen to her. Shay realized sometimes you make choices in life that you don't have the answers to. What she felt with Kareem, she never had with Ronnie. They were two different people at totally different ends of the spectrum. Shay loved Kareem, and she would never apologize for feeling the way she did towards him. She wanted Ronnie to be a part of his son's life, but she wasn't going to make any concessions in her relationship with Kareem. Ronnie seeing his son and Kareem being in her life didn't go hand in hand. It was something Ronnie would have to come to accept. What the two of them once had was over.

Shay lay on her bed, thinking. A few moments later, she pulled out her phone and texted Ronnie. It was weird for her since she hadn't initiated a text to him in a long time.

She simply texted, *What did you do?*

It took all of about a few minutes for him to respond.

What's going on, Shay? Where's my son?

Shay grew agitated. She knew Ronnie was only asking for Jaxson because he was using him to get back in with her, trying to make her believe he wanted them to be a family. Ronnie was being the typical selfish dude that she knew him to be. Ronnie was like every other man; he didn't realize what he had until he saw her with someone else.

Oh, where's your little boyfriend? LOL!

His text further upset Shay because Ronnie was taunting her. She decided to get straight to the point.

Yo, Ronnie, who's Charles?

Asking that question made Ronnie furious because it seemed like Shay was more worried about her boyfriend than letting him see his son.

I'll tell you as soon as you let me see my son, Shayla. All I want to do is see my son.

Shay sat thinking long and hard. If she let Ronnie see his son, would he finally leave her alone and give her the information she demanded to help clear Kareem's name? But how would him seeing Jaxson happen? She didn't want Ronnie knowing where she lived, not even the area. She also knew she wasn't going back to Baltimore any time soon. She thought about doing a FaceTime call with Ronnie. That way, Ronnie would see Jaxson, and Jaxson would see his father. Who was she kidding? That would never be enough for Ronnie. He would only continue to demand more than she wanted to give him, but at that point, it was his only option.

I don't plan on coming back no time soon, Ronnie. I have school, and I work on the weekends. Can we schedule a FaceTime call or something?

Shay sat and waited for his reply. A part of her felt like she was giving in to everything he wanted, and he was so unpredictable, even that made her sick.

Finally, he replied, *Fine. Have my son FaceTime me tomorrow.*

That night, Shay struggled to sleep. She felt like she was opening up a can of worms, and she honestly didn't want to deal with Ronnie or his antics.

*****

The next day, Shay continued with her daily routine. It was the weekend, and she was on her way to work. Her shifts at the hospital weren't long but were enough to give her a few extra dollars to spend on herself and Jaxson. She usually worked five hours.

Before heading out, she made sure Jaxson was fed, changed, and watching TV with Ma. Then she ran and grabbed her bag from behind the door in her room. After kissing Jaxson, Shay told Ma that she would see her in a few hours.

"Alright, baby, have a good day," Ma said before the door closed behind Shay.

Walking to the bus stop, Shay took her usual route, passing Tremont Street and Smith Street. For some reason, she had a funny feeling in her stomach. She felt like someone was following her, but she didn't see anyone whenever she turned around. However, she could've sworn she saw someone from her peripheral view.

Sick people, she thought.

As soon as she passed Tremont, someone grabbed her from behind. Whoever the person was whispered and told her that she shouldn't be surprised because daddy was there. Recognizing the voice, Shay instantly started to sob. It was Ronnie. She wondered how he knew where she was and how long he had been watching her.

Ronnie threw his arm around Shay's shoulders and walked a few steps with her. At the end of the street, he forced her to get into a parked car. Shay's heart began to race. She wanted to run, even scream, but she was afraid of what he would do to her. She had a flashback, remembering the time when he slapped her because she had voiced her opinion. It was the first time he ever hit her, and he vowed it would never happen again.

38

It was Saturday morning, and Kareem was anxious to check in with Shay to see if she had reached out to Ronnie. He knew she worked on Saturdays, so he decided to wait until later to call her. Besides, he just wanted to chill around the house with JaiLynn. He usually worked at the hospital on the weekend or picked up a few hours during the week, but with everything that had been going on, he wanted to relax.

He got out of bed and walked to the bathroom. Passing JaiLynn's room, he saw her watching TV. Saturday mornings were a sleep-in day for everyone in the house. No one got up early, and they all dragged their feet unless there was a need for them to be somewhere.

Once out of the bathroom, Kareem stopped in JaiLynn's room to catch up. JaiLynn annoyed him daily, but she was still his little sister.

"Are you good with everything going on?" she asked him as he sat on the edge of her bed.

"Yeah, I am. I wish this stuff wasn't going on, though," Kareem replied in frustration. "How 'bout you? You know I saw Donté yesterday on the bus. Did he try to reach out to you?"

JaiLynn turned her attention from the TV and looked at Kareem.

"You know it wasn't even like that," JaiLynn replied.

"Then what was it, Jai? I know what I saw," Kareem said, his voice elevated.

"Kareem, you know everything Donté has been through. Answer me this. Did you or Eddie's behavior change with him when y'all started kickin' it with Shay and Renee? Y'all went from being with each other every day to getting girls and dropping him like he was going to kill y'all vibe or something," said JaiLynn.

She went on to tell Kareem how Donté came to the house that night to talk about how he felt about Kareem and Eddie dissing him. She reminded Kareem that Donté didn't do well with change.

A part of Kareem forgot how things were for Donté growing up; he went through a lot.

"Bro, he came to me because I was the next closest person to him outside of you and Eddie. Y'all been keeping him out of the loop. How would you feel? Maybe he thinks that you and Eddie feel like y'all relationships with Renee and Shay are more important than him," JaiLynn explained as she pulled the TV remote from underneath Kareem's thigh.

Kareem stood up and tossed JaiLynn's pillow at her head before walking out the room.

"Dummy!" she yelled.

39

Shay's mind raced, and a tear rolled down her cheek as she tried to see a way out of the mess Ronnie had designed especially for her. She couldn't believe Ronnie was doing this to her. He held her mouth and told her if she screamed or attempted to run, he would get upset.

"Where's my son?" he calmly asked.

Shay cried even harder. She wanted to speak, but she wasn't sure what Ronnie might do. She knew Ronnie was prone to do some questionable things, but she couldn't say she saw anything that would have led her to believe he was capable of kidnapping. Clearly, nothing mattered to Ronnie, especially not his freedom because he was bugging. She wondered to what length this man would go to try to prove his point.

Shay, get it together, she told herself. *If he sees you're weak, he's going to try to use it to his advantage.*

"Ronnie, what the hell are you doing, man?" she asked, finally finding her voice to speak.

"Proving my point. I thought I told you that I wanted my family back," he said.

"What family?" Shay replied, staring at him.

Ronnie quickly lifted his hand as if he were about to palm her face, and she flinched. When he tried to pull her body close to his, she resisted.

"So you really ain't messin' with me, huh?" he asked.

He continued to question Shay without allowing her the opportunity to speak. "You choosing that dude over me?"

"This has nothing to do with him, Ronnie, which makes me wonder why you would try to set him up like that. Your issue is with me. Can't you see that? And we've been done. We are on two different levels. As a matter of fact, where's your new girl? Aren't you expecting another kid?" Shay asked, beginning to stand up to Ronnie.

Her tone changed as flashbacks of Ronnie's abusive behavior resurfaced. She didn't care what he would do. She was going to have her say, and Ronnie wouldn't stop her. Shay started to realize that Ronnie wasn't going to hurt her. Because if that's what he wanted to do, he would have done it already. Upon that realization, Shay's confidence level reached an all-time high.

Soon, she found herself cussing Ronnie's ass out. She was upset that he thought he had control over her. Ronnie failed to realize she was stronger than he thought. So, she had to show him that she ran her own life, and he no longer had a say in how she did things and how she would raise Jaxson.

"Let me explain something to you. My son nor I belong to you. Every day I have choices to make. I get up, take care of my son, and handle my responsibilities. You, on the other hand, continue to run the streets, make more kids, and think you're the cream of the crop. You ain't shit, Ronnie, and I'm sure you'll show my son better than I could ever tell him. If his existence isn't important enough for you to get your shit together, then that's going to be on you," Shay spat, then sighed.

Ronnie was quiet, not knowing how to respond.

"Unlock this damn door, and don't ever come at me like this again. You're lucky I don't have your stupid ass locked up. You want to see my son? Since you're so damn bad, take me to court, bitch! You should have left things how they were, and you would've been seeing your son."

Shay kicked open the door and got out, leaving Ronnie with his mouth wide open. For the first time, he was speechless.

Shay bolted out of the car and ran straight to her house. A part of her didn't want to go home, but at this point, she figured Ronnie already knew where she lived. Her heart was racing, and she was out of breath. All she wanted to do was get home to her son. Once in the house, she immediately locked the doors, grabbed Jaxson from Ma, and began sobbing uncontrollably. She couldn't believe what Ronnie had just done; he tried to make a move on her and hold her against her will.

"What's the matter, baby?" Ma asked, full of concern.

Shay continued to sob but now harder. Ma grew worried. She knew something terrible had to have happened for Shay to come back to the house distraught, when she should have been on her way to work.

"Baby, you're going to have to tell me something," Ma said as she peeked out the living room window.

It took Shay a while before she was able to calm herself down enough to respond to Ma, and when she did, Ma was furious with the stunt Ronnie tried to pull. After moments of trying to explain in detail, Shay called her job and called out, stating a family emergency. Then she called Kareem over. She didn't want to make the mistake of not calling him, and when she did, he raced right to her house.

After receiving the call from Shay, Kareem dressed quickly and went straight to her house. When he arrived, he found Shay extremely upset. Shay was relieved to see Kareem. As they hugged, Kareem reassured Shay that he wasn't going to let anything happen to her or Jaxson. He was devastated to see the fear in her eyes. He had to wonder if Shay had told him everything.

Kareem wanted to find Ronnie and beat the hell out of him for many reasons, but mainly because he had dared to put his hands on Shay. Ronnie had escalated this to a level that they couldn't come back from. Kareem was put in a position where he had to do something; he couldn't let Ronnie get away with what he had done. Ronnie would come to regret that he ever showed up in Richmond. Kareem was stuck, though. Part of him wanted to call up Eddie and put hands on Ronnie. The other part of him had to remember he was a suspect in an ongoing murder case. As Kareem watched Shay nervous in her own home, he made up his mind at that moment. He had to do what he had to do to make sure Shay felt safe. To hell with the investigation. Let the cards fall where they may.

Stepping outside, he called Eddie and told him to meet him at Shay's. Kareem briefly explained everything to Eddie and was waiting for him when he showed up with Donté by his side. Kareem was thrown off by Donté's appearance. At that moment, whatever was going on between them went out the window. They dapped each other up and shared a one-arm hug. All had been forgiven.

"So, what you wanna do?" Eddie asked, down for anything.

"You know I'm always down to ride. How's Shay and little man?" Donté asked Kareem.

"They're cool. I'm keeping my eye on them," Kareem responded. He wasn't surprised at Donté's question. Although a week ago, Kareem would have read more into it.

Kareem, Donté, and Eddie sat in Shay's kitchen and talked about what they were going to do. Ma had gone to church. She told Shay that she needed to be in the Lord's house to pray over this mess. Shay lay on the couch in the living room with Jaxson. She was asleep in no time, and Kareem watched her as she slumbered. When her breathing became even, he knew she was in a deep sleep. That's when he picked up her phone from the coffee table and searched for Ronnie's number. Once he got the number, he put her phone back.

"Bro, you got the code to her phone?" Eddie asked, not believing Kareem could access the number so quickly.

"That's my girl. What she got to hide?" Kareem responded, with a look that said did he really have to tell Eddie that.

Together, they planned how they were going to set Ronnie up. First, they had to find out if he was still in town. Kareem felt like he was still in Richmond since his main mission was to try to win Shay back and see Jaxson.

Kareem called Ronnie's number. He didn't know what he was going to say, but he knew it wasn't going to be good once he got him on the phone. The phone rang and rang. Right before Kareem was about to hang up, Ronnie answered.

"Yo, I see you on some real bullshit. But you messed up when you came for mine," Kareem angrily told him.

"Who is this?" Ronnie replied.

"You know who this is. The next time you wanna do something to me, partna, step to me like a man," Kareem said.

He wanted to get Ronnie upset enough that he would agree to meet him. Then he would give Ronnie the ass whooping he should have given him in his hometown.

Donté and Eddie sat back while Kareem grew angrier while talking to Ronnie. Before they knew it, Kareem was giving Ronnie an address to meet him to settle things. The address he gave Ronnie was next to a local abandoned park near the train tracks. Eddie called his older cousin to give them a ride to the park. Kareem planned to leave once Ma got back to the house so Shay wouldn't be alone.

*****

By the time they arrived at the park, it was sunset. Kareem was the only one who got out of the car. Eddie, Donté, and Eddie's cousin waited in the car parked behind the stone bridge columns. The plan was to ambush Ronnie and whoever came with him. The car was loaded with two steel baseball bats and a crowbar. None of them had guns, but they knew how to handle their business. The plan wasn't to kill Ronnie; they only wanted to make him wish he were dead.

Ronnie was sitting on a bench on the far right of the abandoned park. The grass was overgrown, and trash and empty liquor bottles littered the ground from the homeless who slept there every night. No one frequented the area much besides the nightwalkers and bums. So, it was the perfect place to leave someone bruised and battered.

Kareem didn't see anyone with Ronnie, but that didn't mean he was alone. He could have been pulling the same stunt as Kareem.

"You had a lotta mouth on the phone," Ronnie sneered.

"Still do, bitch."

"I'ma tell you this one time, bitch-ass nigga! Stay away from my family!" Ronnie yelled, pointing his finger in Kareem's face.

"You got me all the way fucked up, nigga! You ain't got no family to stay away from, motherfucker!" Kareem shouted.

That was the button to push to set things in motion. Ronnie swung at Kareem, striking him in the jaw. Kareem came back with a quick right to Ronnie's eye. He went down on his knee.

"Now I'm going to give you the ass whooping your mammy should have given you a long time ago," Kareem told him, before commencing to doing exactly what he said.

The two tussled in the park for about five minutes until blood was shed. Kareem had a busted forehead, and Ronnie's nose was shifted. It didn't take Eddie and Donté long to come from the corner of the park. When that happened, another unidentified person came from out the cut, too. Donté swung the bat at the guy, while Eddie ran over to where Kareem was and gave Ronnie his fair share. The three boys decided Ronnie had enough when he lay on the concrete unconscious in a fetal position. The dude who had attempted to run to Ronnie's aid ended up badly beaten up, too. Donté must have had a lot of pent-up frustration, because the guy laid on the ground limp before trying to crawl to the bench and use it to get his balance.

Before they left the park, Kareem leaned down and whispered in Ronnie's ear, "Looks like you've been counted out, youngblood. Stay away from my girl. She's through with you. Oh, and another thing, you're lucky killing ain't my motivation because I would've sent your no-good ass to see ya boy, Charles."

As Kareem walked away, Ronnie tried to respond but couldn't. Donté and Eddie dashed to the car, not wanting to be spotted by anyone.

"Man, who's Charles?" Eddie asked once they were back inside the car and pulling off.

On their way back to the neighborhood, Kareem explained what happened to him a couple of nights prior. When Kareem got home, he called Shay to check on her after cleaning the cut on his forehead. He told her about the events that occurred at the park. To his surprise, she did not question him or ask if Ronnie was okay. Shay knew Kareem didn't kill him, and in her eyes, Ronnie needed a good beatdown. Shay slept better that night knowing Ronnie wasn't going to pop up on her.

41

The next day, Kareem told Shay that he would stop by after work. He also told her that she didn't have to worry about Ronnie anymore, which comforted her to hear. Everything that was going on did not sit well with Ma, though. So, she called one of those home security companies to have them come and install a camera outside of the building and in the hall. She wanted to be sure Ronnie or no one else would pop up on them uninvited. That one encounter was enough. Despite Ma's urging, Shay didn't go to the police. What would she say? Her son's father wanted to see his son and she wouldn't let him? Everything was so complicated.

The next day, Renee came by to hang with Shay and Jaxson. Shay didn't want to go out of the house. Plus, at this point, the only one she felt safe with was Kareem.

"You love him?" Renee asked.

Shay took a minute to look at her friend. She tried to avoid the question, and even though she was stubborn enough not to confess anything, her heart said something else. A single tear slid down Shay's face as she slowly looked up at Renee, who was holding Jaxson.

"Awwww, Shay, it's okay to feel that way. You should never deny how you feel. If you deny it, you will only hurt yourself. You don't have to say anything for me to know. I'm your best friend. I already know," Renee said.

Shay wiped away the tears that wet her face and smiled. Shay's heart was relieved that someone else knew how she felt about Kareem. He was going to bat for her. No one had ever done that for her before, and she appreciated it. Even when she was with Ronnie, his actions were never as strong as this. He caused her more pain than happiness.

Shay sat and reflected with Renee about everything she had been through in the past year—from having Jaxson, moving to a new state, the mess with Ronnie, making new friends, and meeting Kareem. With it being her senior year of high school, she should have been focused on her future plans. Instead, she couldn't help but think what would occur in the next few days.

A few weeks had passed since everything happened, and things appeared to be quiet. However, Kareem was still dealing with the homicide investigation. It would have been easy for Kareem to tell the police that Ronnie was the person who implicated him. But, like other young boys, he stuck to the code of not snitching. Kareem didn't see it like that, though, because he felt the detectives would uncover the truth. And they finally did.

One day, Kareem and his lawyer got a call for them to come to the police station. When he, his mother, and his attorney arrived at the police station, the detectives informed Kareem that cellular data didn't put him anywhere in the area at the time of Charles's death. Therefore, Kareem was no longer considered a suspect in the murder. Even though Kareem was relieved not to have his name connected to the investigation, he still wanted to know how he passed away. Ronnie was a grease ball, one of those Rico from *Paid in Full* type of dudes.

Things were back to normal for the most part. There had been no incidents since the situation with Ronnie, and Kareem was starting to put it all behind him. However, every time he saw Jaxson, he was reminded that Ronnie was his father.

The school year was coming to an end, and Kareem hoped to get into a tech program so he could focus on his trade. Shay applied to a few local schools, too. Kareem and Shay's relationship had grown stronger since everything transpired. In fact, everyone's relationship was better. They all hung out and even included Donté, despite him being the fifth wheel. Whenever they went out, they tried to scout him out a girl to kick it with so he wouldn't have to be alone.

After that incident with Ronnie pulling up on Shay, Ma decided to take her to work each day. Shay hadn't heard anything from him. She didn't even know if he was okay since that beating he got.

Shay and Kareem often texted each other while at work. Their workdays seemed long despite them not actually being long. But they passed the time with texting. On this day, Shay's sister, Jaylah, texted her.

Hey, Mama wants to know if Ronnie came to see you and Jaxson.

Shay sat there in shock, with all types of thoughts running through her mind. Why would her mother ask her that? Furthermore, she didn't even talk to her mother like that, so why would she care? Then, it hit her. She questioned the scene with Ronnie repeatedly in her head, and the question she always asked herself was how he knew where she lived. But, at that moment, she knew it must have been her mother.

Taking a break, Shay went to the bathroom to call her mother.

"Ma, did Ronnie tell you that he was coming to see the baby and me?" Shay asked.

"Well, hello to you, too. You know better than to call my phone and not say hi or nothing—just start asking questions," her mother replied.

Before Shay could respond, her mother told her how Ronnie came to her house a few weeks back. He asked her for Shay's address because he wanted to surprise Shay and the baby since he hadn't seen them since he got out of jail. Shay was furious because he set her mother up, and not knowing what was going on between them, her mother told him where Shay lived.

"Ma, do you know Ronnie came to Ma's house and attacked me? I don't deal with Ronnie, Mama. Why didn't you call me first? Why would you tell him where I live?" Shay asked, upset.

The phone went silent. For the first time, her mother didn't know what to say besides she was sorry. Before her mother could get her words together, Shay hung up on her. After she got off the phone with her, Shay called her sister and told her everything. She had held off telling her everything that was going on to avoid scaring her and having her worry. But telling her after the fact still had Jaylah worried.

Shay was hurt but couldn't blame her mother simply because she didn't talk like that with her. Therefore, her mother wouldn't have known anything. But, moving forward, her mother would now know.

Later that night, Jaylah called Shay to tell her that their father had to bail their mother out of jail. Jaylah reported that her mother went to Ronnie's mother's house because she assumed he stayed there. Their mother cussed out Ronnie's mother, and she called the police because she felt threatened. Jaylah went on to tell her that their mother cussed out Ronnie's sister, too. Shay was happy her mother gave Ronnie a piece of her mind but knew she had to call her mother and tell her to chill out before things really got out of control. Shay didn't want her mother to be cussing out Ronnie's mother every time she saw her. Ronnie's mother wasn't the problem; he was.

Shay explained everything to Kareem, who was just as shocked as she was upon hearing what Shay's mother had done. But there was nothing for anyone to do since they hadn't heard anything more from Ronnie. Things seemed to be going smoothly…until the day came.

44

Still focused in school, Kareem put forth more of an effort. He wasn't doing it only to prove to himself that he could be successful, but also to prove it to people like Mr. Washington and even his uncle Mike. He had been through a lot, but he made it too far to stop pushing. So, he sent off his applications for vocational schools in the area so he could move forward with studying electrical work.

Spring vacation came, and right before Kareem was about to go back to school on Monday, he came home from work on Sunday night to see two envelopes from two local schools. Attached to the top envelope was a sticky note with the message *Good Luck ~ Mom!* Kareem was too nervous to open the envelopes because he was afraid of rejection. So, he walked by the letters and headed to the shower. When he got out of the shower, he immediately called Shay, who reported that she was studying for a math exam she had the next day. When he told her about the letters, Shay appeared to be more excited than he was about getting them. She sensed something was up because he became quiet. That's when she decided she would FaceTime him to see his face.

"Reem, open the letters, bae. If you didn't get accepted, it doesn't mean you give up. You just apply to other programs," Shay said, trying to encourage him to open the letters.

Kareem sat on the end of his bed, looking at Shay on his phone's screen. He was more focused on what she was doing than the mail.

"Reem, open the mail," Shay pleaded. "I'm anxious."

Kareem reached over and grabbed the letters off his nightstand. He opened the first one and started to read it.

Dear Kareem,
Congratulations! We would like to extend the opportunity for you to come interview with us at the school to see if you would like to move forward with attending our school.

With a smile on his face, he opened the second letter, which read something similar.

"Bae, you got in! You got in!" Shay shouted.

Kareem yelled out in excitement, waking everyone in the house. Thinking something was wrong, his mother rushed into his room. When he explained that he got accepted into the schools, she was overjoyed. She extended her arms to give her son the biggest hug as a tear rolled down her cheek.

"Stop limiting your abilities. I knew you would get in. I'm happy you got what you wanted. So, who are we choosing?" she asked.

Words couldn't express how Kareem felt. He knew this was only the beginning, as he had many plans for his future. He was on his way to being a businessman.

45

Shay was so happy for Kareem. She supported him in his decisions just as he did for her. Wanting to do something for Kareem to celebrate his vocational options, she decided to call up Donté and Eddie, and the three of them planned to do something that following Tuesday. They invited Torrie, Uncle Mike, Coach Ellis, JaiLynn, Renee, Ma, Jaxson, and a few of his coworkers. Shay knew this was a big thing for Kareem, as he wasn't interested in college but rather attending an alternative school. At the moment, he knew starting his own business was equally beneficial.

Kareem appreciated everyone who came out to celebrate with him. Since it was a school night, they didn't stay out too late, but Shay wanted to do something sooner rather than wait for the weekend because they both intended to work. In the midst of celebrating with Kareem, Shay was still waiting to see if she got into any of the colleges she sent applications. She also applied for a few scholarships for single mothers.

It seemed as if Kareem and Shay were both on their way. Despite how good things had been going, Shay still had a knot in her stomach. She got that feeling again like something wasn't right.

Later that night, after putting Jaxson in bed, she lay on her bed, scrolling Facebook and trying to catch up on nothing. All of a sudden, she got a text from a random number.

Never sleep on the sleeping beast. It's not over.

She already knew who it was; it was Ronnie. At that point, she knew her life would do a 360. Too much had happened. He was still upset about not seeing his son, and he wanted "his" family back. Then everything that happened with Kareem, Donté, and Eddie only complicated things more. She knew he was coming back.

Once again, Shay was stuck and didn't know what to do. Part of her wanted to call Kareem, but he was celebrating a new beginning, and she didn't want to damper his mood.

A tear rolled down her face as she went over and picked up Jaxson, who was asleep in his crib. Placing him in the bed with her, she held on to her son extra tight that night. Shay knew the decisions she would have to make would ultimately affect him.

Part 2 Coming Soon

Made in the USA
Middletown, DE
25 October 2020